Andrew Dicker retired from a 30 year career in the NHS and embarked on a writing project, because it is something he had always wanted to do, but never had the time until now. His main reason for writing is because he finds it enjoyable and absorbing. He lives in Buckinghamshire.

To Niki
With love
Andrew.

For Alison, with love.

Andrew Dicker

The Seduction of Celia

A Collection of Short Stories

Austin Macauley
Publishers Ltd.

A CIP catalogue record for this title is available from the British Library.

ISBN 9781785548178 (Paperback)
ISBN 9781785548185 (Hardback)
ISBN 9781785548192 (E-Book)

www.austinmacauley.com

First Published (2016)
Austin Macauley Publishers Ltd.
25 Canada Square
Canary Wharf
London
E14 5LQ

Contents

Lucinda

Plant fairs are popular events in English villages. They bring the neighbours together on sunny, Sunday mornings. The neighbours stand in clumps on the village green gossiping about each other and the next social event at the pub or the village hall.

People who are not part of the neighbourhood are conspicuously uninvolved in the parochial introspection. They have, after all, come to buy plants, and probably driven from neighbouring villages. The plants are usually small and designed for hanging baskets or pots. Among the rows of propagated seedlings are a few more exotic specimens, maybe intended to be house plants. The sellers behind the stalls are amateur greenhouse enthusiasts, out to make a few pounds on a Sunday morning.

Having bought a dozen very small plants, which would be sufficient to create a colourful effect in the big earthenware pots which had accumulated, over the years, outside the kitchen door, I wandered about the grassy fair, observing the small family outings in the refreshment tent. Aged parents had been wheeled out for a cup of tea and a creamy confection in the middle of the morning. I was not paying attention to the direction of my wandering and stood on something uneven in the grass. Too late I realised that the object was a foot which belonged to a woman who, I suspect, was paying equally little attention to her itinerary, or she would not have left her foot in my path.

I apologised as sincerely as I could think how. I looked at the foot which was clad in a neat, clean trainer. Then I looked at the face of the owner of the foot. She had short, dark hair, kept off her face with a blue hair band, pale skin and a nose slightly too large for the rest of her face. Her mouth was small and her eyes large and dark. Her eyes were too close together and upset the symmetry of her face. There was something extraordinary about her eyes which were particularly bright. I realised the effect was because her pupils were widely dilated, despite the bright, spring light.

'Not to worry,' she said, 'no harm done.'

'You must be a gardener,' I volunteered, 'or you wouldn't be here.'

'Actually no; I came to see what a plant fair is. I've never been to one before, being a bit of a townie. I was thinking about pots for my balcony.'

'What d'you make of it?'

'It seems to be a village event – definitely not for outsiders. But it's quaint, I suppose.' She sounded disappointed. I looked at her huge eyes again and wondered if my pupils were the same size as hers. It is paradoxical, I thought, that although we constantly look through our pupils we never know what they are doing, or what messages they might be conveying to other people. I wondered if she knew how striking her eyes were. We meandered along aimlessly and spontaneously. She was a few inches shorter than me. She wore a loose black tee-shirt and black, skinny jeans. All rather understated, as if she did not want to be noticed. It struck me that we were wearing identical clothes. I decided to see if we had anything else in common.

'Have you come far?'

'About ten miles.' She named the nearest market town.

‘I live in the next village, about three miles away.’ I hesitated. ‘D’you like cheese?’ I wondered how silly my question sounded.

‘Yes,’ she said, and added, to my surprise, ‘as long as it’s English.’ Another thing we had in common.

‘I need to get back’ I said, ‘I left the bread in the oven. Do you want to come and have some English cheese to compensate for having your foot trodden on?’

‘Why not? As long as it really is English’. We headed for the car park at the edge of the green. She got into a small, new-looking car and followed me through the lanes to where I lived.

Our small convoy arrived at my house, where I had lived alone for some time. It is large and meant for a family, who were all departed. I hurried into the kitchen to rescue the bread, leaving the doors open behind me for my guest to follow. She followed me into the kitchen where I was burning my hands on the new loaf, as I extracted it hastily from the oven.

‘I’m Michael,’ I said. ‘What are you called?’

‘Lucinda. I get called Lucy or Linda or even Cindy, but I prefer Lucinda.’

‘Lucinda. A pretty name. I don’t like contractions either; Mike being the worst thing you can call me.’

I started to arrange lumps of cheese on the board; Lancashire, Stilton, a red looking one with blue veins, of which I had forgotten the name, and crumbling Cheddar.

‘Glass of wine?’

‘Thank you’ said Lucinda as she accepted a glass of claret. ‘D’you work locally?’ I asked.

‘Not really. I moved to a flat not far from here. I’ve been living alone for six months to escape a lot of things that went rather badly. I work in North London. I do a sort of commute to work, which is the only part of life which has gone well. Life is otherwise deliberately dull, so accepting invitations to eat cheese with a stranger is a wild adventure.'

There was a wounded note in her story which invited enquiry, but I was not sure that intrusion would be welcome. 'What's the work?'

'I'll tell you my boring routine. Wake up, having slept badly. Get up. Drink something. Pack office clothes in a small rucksack. Put on Lycra kit. Run two miles to the station. Half an hour on the train. Run one more mile to the office. Shower. Change into work clothes. Work at a computer for a small start-up company. Do meetings. More computering. Change back into running kit. Run one mile to the station. Half an hour on the train. Run two miles back to the flat. Shower. Eat. Drink sometimes. Read. TV. Back to bed. Sleep badly.'

'Why can't you sleep?'

'I'm better at it than I was. I think I was probably depressed. Exercise has been the most helpful thing.'

I looked at her. She was of an indeterminate age, maybe forty. She was lean, like an athlete, beneath the tee-shirt. There was a gamine litheness about her. She noticed me inspecting her. 'Yes' she said, 'I know, I've lost too much weight. Actually I rather like it. I think it's good for self-esteem, of which I have been rather short'.

She seemed to beg so many questions. I was not going to get involved but I felt that I should acknowledge that there was a problem, or had been.

'You sound as if you've been through a rough time.' I said tentatively.

'I'll tell you about it, if you like, but I think I should know who it is I am telling'. We sat at the kitchen table inspecting the cheese and the cooling loaf.

I explained that I was retired, earlier than I had anticipated, after countless years' work as a GP. The children had grown up and left. My partner had left as well and gone to live in France with someone she had met. What I did now was what I might have done, many years ago, had I not done what I did. The only structured part of the day was learning to write fiction. The rest of the time I wandered about the countryside, sometimes drawing landscapes, and socialising. I went to London at intervals to be a tourist, because I had not had a chance to do any of that while I continued to work. 'It's a rather sedentary existence, but contented,' I concluded.

'Lucky you,' said Lucinda.

A silence lodged itself between us. I had the sense that we would either have to invent small talk or I was about to hear a confession. Having listened to people's narratives for decades, I knew intuitively how to allow people to say what they needed to say; I was an expert listener. A frown passed over Lucinda's face trying to decide to tell or not to tell. I raised my eyebrows interrogatively. Smiling rather unconvincingly, she stared at the cheese board for a while and then inhaled deeply, unsure whether to smile or cry.

'I don't know why but I think I can trust you. I'm going to tell you what happened.'

I stood up to fetch the bottle, which I thought might help. 'What sort of thing happened to you?' I asked.

'A relationship which went wrong; more than wrong. It was horrible. I'm not over it yet, so I'm taking a risk by trying to talk about it. I might get upset.' She fixed her huge, dark eyes on me. I reflected her gaze and smiled, encouragingly, I hoped.

'A few years ago I met this man. We seemed to get on and eventually started to live together in his house in London. He worked in the city and was well off. We had a very regulated life, doing the same things week in and week out. It suited me in many ways. My job was going well and I worked an awful lot of hours, so having an uncomplicated home life was fine, or so I thought. We seemed to adopt roles in the house like cooking, cleaning, doing the laundry, loading the dish-washer, looking after the very small garden. But if something was not done he became impatient and then critical. He seemed to take everything for granted, particularly the things which I was apparently supposed to do for him, like ironing his shirts and, on one occasion, cleaning his shoes. Slowly it became stifling. I started to anticipate his expectations, which was easier than waiting for him to point out my failings, which was how it felt. We still managed to have quite a good time together, going out, entertaining; but there was this constant intolerance of things which were not exactly to his liking. I felt less and less appreciated.'

She stopped and considered where the story was going. She ceased eye contact with me and studied the cheese board again. 'And then there was the sex.' I waited. Lucinda started to talk rapidly, as if she needed to get it over with as quickly as possible.

'I know now that sex is the corner-stone of any relationship. If it doesn't work, or doesn't happen, you might as well pack it in. Actually I used to like sex; almost anything can be forgiven with real intimacy. But sex in our relationship was all about him. He decided when and what. The worst thing was that it was always exactly the same and completely unimaginative. I got fucked then he went to sleep, so to speak. With hindsight, I think that deciding to confront him about how bad our sex had become was a serious misjudgement. But I did, in bed one night, about six months ago. I thought I had tried to be empathetic and talked about us, not just him. I realise now that criticism of any sort was something he couldn't cope with, and with something as sensitive as sex it was a disaster. He sat up in bed, turned around and slapped me hard on my face. It took me completely by surprise. I sat on the edge of the bed holding my face. He got up, came around to my side of the bed and hit me again so hard I briefly lost consciousness. The next thing I knew I was being held face down on the bed with an awful pain in my face and an equally bad pain somewhere in my pelvis.' Lucinda paused, inhaled deeply and continued without looking at me. 'He'd managed to stick his thing in my bum and was grunting and groaning.' Lucinda looked up at me briefly, reached for her glass and swallowed hard before continuing.

'It was horrible and sadistic. As I came to, it dawned on me that I was being raped and the horror of it brought me round. I screamed and struggled but that seemed to excite him more, judging by the animal noises coming from him. Then suddenly it was over. I got away from him, grabbed my jeans and a tee-shirt, locked myself in the bathroom and waited. Everything went silent so I crept out, found my phone and door-key and left. It was about one o'clock in the morning and freezing. I ran for ages through the streets to the house of a friend, who took me in.'

Lucinda stopped talking. Huge tears welled up over her eye-lids and ran down her cheeks. I reached for the kitchen role which I used for napkins, tore off a couple of sheets and handed them to her. She hid her face behind the paper and sobbed convulsively for a minute or two. Having been in this situation countless times, in a professional role, I knew that she needed time and space to deal with the overwhelming effect of relating these ghastly events. I was uncertain if physical contact would be appropriate so I gazed out of the window, acutely feeling her misery, and thought I might become tearful as well. The worst of the emotional turmoil ebbed and receded.

'I'm so sorry' she said, haltingly, 'I really am. I have no right to be dumping all this on you. Where's the loo?' I pointed her in the right direction. After a while she reappeared looking composed and smiling. 'I'm embarrassed now,' she said.

'Don't be daft. It takes a lot of courage to talk like this and I want to know what happened next, if it's OK with you'. The atmosphere was strained and awkward and I wanted to make it more ordinary.

'You're being really kind but I think it does help to talk. It's the first time, apart from with my friend who rescued me on the night. Actually there's not much more to say.' She drained her glass and I refilled it.

'In the morning my face was terribly bruised and my friend wanted me to go to the police or the doctor. I couldn't face the prospect. More than anything, I wanted to do something to sever every contact with my now ex-partner. We both phoned in sick and then went on a mission to raid the house to retrieve my possessions. He'd gone to work, as if nothing had happened. No message. No remorse. I realised that I didn't actually own much apart from clothes. It was as if the things in the house were all possessed by him, me included. I stuffed the clothes in super-market bags and couldn't think of anything else that I could legitimately call mine. I was desperate to leave. I slammed the door and stuck the keys through the letter box, as a sort of gesture of finality.'

The pace of Lucinda's story had slowed and I felt a palpable sense of relief. Descriptions of brutality always made me feel tense and helpless. I hoped she was not going to tell me that the man had come after her. We sat companionably in silence with the wine, nibbling the remnants of the cheese. It was not difficult to see that Lucinda had been terribly hurt and was far from recovered, or even approaching some sort of acceptance of the vileness of her partner's behaviour. I sensed there were more tears on the way so I moved the kitchen paper closer to her. She hauled a great length off the role and buried her face in it.

After a while she lowered the kitchen role screen and looked at me with dark, soulful eyes over the top of the crumpled paper. 'I'm hopeless,' she announced and giggled slightly.

'Far from it. You've been traumatised; it takes courage to talk about this sort of thing. I don't believe that most people can cope with abuse alone. Tell me how it feels to have told a stranger about it?' I could hear my professional self behind the conversation.

'It feels lovely talking to you. You don't feel like a stranger. Although may be it helps that you are. Being listened to is a good feeling; acts of kindness always make me emotional. But you're right, I think I am traumatised, more than I want to acknowledge. The recollection of his hand bashing into my face, and what he did afterwards, is vivid and horrible. I don't know how to get rid of it.'

'You just made a start,' I said emphatically, looking at her steadily.

'What saved me from penury, or the abused women's hostel, was having money. I get well paid and my job really is interesting. It distracted me completely and allowed a sort of recovery, but I know I'm still vulnerable. I stayed with my friend for less than a week. I found the flat, where I'm living now, almost immediately. It was unfurnished, but with views over the neighbouring houses to the fields, and a balcony. I organised a shipping order from IKEA and spent the next two weeks struggling with Alan keys and screw-drivers. Best of all, no one knew where I was, apart from my rescue friend. For several months work saved me. I couldn't enjoy anything, particularly socialising. I couldn't eat or sleep and was exhausted all the time. Oddly, work and running were all that I could do energetically. I think it's slowly coming right now but the scars in my memory of that night need some sort of cauterising. I think it was so unexpected. It took me completely by surprise. I had no idea he was capable of being so brutal and sadistic. I suppose he felt threatened by having his sexual performance questioned. How fragile men are.'

'Have you thought about seeing a therapist or psychologist, or someone?' I asked tentatively.

'I think I'll be OK. The nights are the worst, but not as bad as they were. I used to lie awake for hours ruminating about how it happened. It made me feel disgusting. I managed to convince myself that I smelled repulsive. Some nights I couldn't stop crying. I even felt guilty because it had been my fault for wanting to talk about sex. The memory is not as raw as it was and sometimes I even sleep normally.'

My professional self knew that there was one more question which I should ask. 'D'you ever think about doing anything to yourself, harmful I mean?'

Lucinda smiled weakly. 'There speaks the doctor.' She said. There was a pause. 'Yes. I used to, during the worst nights. When the sense of self-disgust was all I could think about, it used to seem impossible that I could ever be acceptable to anyone again. And yes, I thought, this is why people kill themselves. I really did think about it for hours. Eventually I would sleep and in the morning it all seemed unlikely, and I could not think how to do it, even if I really wanted to. I think I'm over that now.' She smiled again, I think to reassure me.

Our frugal lunch was over. Lucinda decided that she needed to return to her flat to do things. Before she left I insisted that she took my phone numbers. 'It's a great relief that things seem to be better,' I said, 'but if it gets worse again and you need someone to talk to, call me, please.'

'Just being listened to helps,' she said, 'you're good at that.'

'I've had a lot of practice.'

I did not really expect to hear from her. Her life would slowly get back to normal but I did not think it could ever be the same for her as before the events she had related. I suspected it would affect her in all sorts of unforeseen ways as time went by. The weeks passed in a leisurely way, and what I came to think about as the plant fair affair, faded from memory.

A few months later I was visiting the village shop, rather late in the day, in the hope that there was a newspaper left. They had all been sold apart from the local county news-sheet. I glanced at the headline: 'Suicide woman named.' I sensed the inevitability of what came next before I read on. 'The woman found hanging from her balcony, in the early hours of Tuesday morning, has been named as Lucinda…'

Billy's Story

Billy was born a junkie.

Martha, his Mum, was a junkie too. She was twenty years old when she had Billy, four weeks before he was due.

Martha had a rotten childhood, left school without passing any exams and met a dealer who taught her to inject herself with heroin. She sank into junkie life, minor criminality and occasional street work, to pay for her habit. She cleaned up more than once but relapse was always round the corner. Substitute prescribing worked for Martha. She could get off the heroin quite easily. The problem was staying off. Craving was a constant anxiety.

The way Billy was conceived went like this.

During a clean spell Martha was obliged to attend the rehab clinic daily to meet her key-worker and sit in groups of recovering junkies, all with the same story of self-recrimination. Her craving never went away. In fact, being in the presence of ex-users made the craving worse. The chat was full of reminders. So when an old dealer acquaintance knocked on the door of her bed-sit, carrying bags of heroin, she let him in. She had no money but she knew from experience that he would supply her in exchange for sex. The dealer put the hit together and left the filled syringe on the bed-side table with a tourniquet, provocatively. He lay on his back, half clothed, and made her sit astride him with his cock inside her. He handed her the tourniquet which she wrapped around her arm. Then he found a vein in her forearm and injected her. A few weeks with no drugs in her system had allowed her tolerance to all but disappear. As she released the tourniquet, she knew that she had been over-dosed as the hit flooded her body and brain with warmth, and then more or less deprived her of consciousness. She felt herself being rolled over. Then the dealer raped her. He left hours later, having made sure Martha was breathing, because he wanted her alive and clucking tomorrow. He found her door keys and phone and locked the door from the outside.

Martha woke hours later, naked on the bed, in a freezing sweat, aching and desperate for the loo. She went back to bed and tried to sleep but the withdrawal was acute. In due course she dragged herself out of bed intending to go out and score again. There was no other way to relieve her misery. Then she realised that she had been locked in her own bedsit and her phone was missing. She also knew who had the keys and what would happen next.

Hours later the dealer returned. Martha was ill. Sex seemed a small price to pay for the next hit. This time he threw the gear on the table with a syringe and a needle from the exchange, and left, locking her in again. She became a prisoner in her bedsit, raped every day for a week in exchange for a bag of heroin and a clean needle. On the eighth day the dealer raped her, dropped her door keys and phone on the table and disappeared without leaving any gear.

Withdrawal consumed Martha's consciousness. She had lived on sweet tea for a week. She was unwashed, bedraggled, thin as a rake, and smelled of her own stale sweat. Her sense of self-disgust was overwhelming. She was too weak to rage against her abuser or her addiction. Loathing her circumstances she knew she must get help. She prised herself from the bed, pulled on her grimy jeans and a crumpled tee-shirt, grabbed the door keys and started to walk to the clinic because there was no money for fares.

She made it to the clinic where the receptionist recognised she was in a crisis. Slowly she was processed through the system to see the doctor who was meticulous in his questioning about what had happened. Martha knew that honesty was the only approach to take. They always found out sooner or later. Had she been to the police? Was she prepared to say who her abuser had been? It was in everyone's interest; who did she think he might be raping now? Eventually they gave her a small dose of methadone, after testing a urine sample and offering a host of other screening tests, which Martha declined; she could not face the possible results.

Her key-worker found her, gave her money and sandwiches and agreed to start all over again. She would attend the clinic daily for a gradually increasing dose of methadone until she was comfortable. The pharmacist had to watch her swallow each daily dose. Weeks went by and Martha was trapped in the boredom of dependency, still craving at each reminder that heroin was readily available on the street.

She survived the next few weeks, obediently keeping appointments. One morning she left the clinic and headed for the bedsit, as usual, but was suddenly overcome with nausea and threw up the methadone in the gutter. Panic set in. There would be no more methadone until tomorrow when she would be withdrawing again. She went back to the clinic and pleaded. The questioning resumed. When did she last have a period? Her periods had stopped months ago; she had thought nothing of it. The inevitable truth dawned on her, confirmed by another urine test a few minutes later.

That was how Billy was conceived. He nearly was not born because Martha's first thought was to get an abortion. As the days went by her ambivalence grew. She realised that perhaps a baby would be a reason for living and getting her life back to normal. The main obstacle to overcome was her poisonous loathing of the father. She spoke to the doctors at the clinic who said pregnancy was better without opiates but the drugs were not particularly harmful. She would have to stay on her steady dose if she wanted to keep the baby and detox after it was born. The baby would be born addicted to Martha's methadone and would need to spend time in the special care unit because of the risk of fits. Billy became the means to the end of keeping Martha off the streets and away from her user acquaintances. She became a model junkie, attending the innumerable appointments which seemed to have become necessary to monitor her pregnancy. She lost her starved, bedraggled look, started to gain weight and began to feel happy. The social services promised her a new flat before the baby arrived.

Early in the morning on the day Billy came into the world Martha was woken by a searing pain somewhere in her pelvis. She sat on the bed holding the tense bump in her tummy and realised the bed was soaking. Her waters had broken four weeks too soon. Martha showered, dressed, gathered her overnight things and took herself straight to the hospital.

The pain was unceasing, not at all like the contractions she had been told to expect in the ante-natal classes. The midwives and doctors poked about. She had another ultra-sound. They told her the baby was going to be born soon.

Billy slithered into the world in a pool of blood and amniotic fluid. He was tiny, yellow, jittery, and addicted to his Mum's methadone. The doctors cloistered him in a plastic incubator wired up to all sorts of machines with tubes dangling everywhere. He had to be sedated to prevent him from fitting until the methadone wore off. Martha was allowed to hold him but could not feed him. She had to be taught to express her milk so Billy could be fed it from a bottle. He was so small he could barely suck.

Within a week Billy had gained weight and grown perceptibly. The nurses disconnected him from the machines, hauled him out of the incubator, wrapped him in a towel and plonked him in Martha's arms. They went back to the bedsit because the promised flat had not materialised.

So that was Billy's start in life; born prematurely to a junkie Mum, living in the most deprived housing in the city and reliant on state benefits.

Billy was a fretful baby. He sensed his mother's tension and rarely settled for long, day or night. Martha was soon exhausted. Her medicalised addiction necessitated regular contact with the clinic and social services, who rapidly understood that she was barely coping. This added to her anxiety as she knew that the authority figures, with whom she had to engage, had the power to take Billy away from her. However much he vexed her Martha was powerfully attached to Billy. Her maternal sense was strong; she was young and energetic. As long as she kept away from heroin she would survive. She was painfully aware of her craving which became worse as the doctors gradually reduced her substitute dose. If she lost her son she would relapse and probably try to kill herself.

Months passed. Billy grew. There was never any money. Martha's main social contact was at the clinic and the numerous visits by the social services. She felt trapped in the rigmarole of the treatment of her addiction. Her mood was fractious and irritable. She became gradually more impatient with Billy, consciously restraining herself whenever she was in the presence of a member of the caring professions. She knew it was only a matter of time before she did something bad to him when he would not settle or caused another of his regular spillages. Despite the adversity of her circumstances, the increasing vulnerability she felt because of her craving and the relentless attention of the social services, she survived the most harrowing months until Billy was mobile and starting to talk. Life seemed less on the edge, the social services relaxed their vigilance and Martha's anxiety lessened. Soon Billy was at nursery and forging his own toddler social life. Martha met the other mums and began to feel that there was more to life than just coping with addiction. But the craving never went away and the streets and the dealers were only the other side of the front door.

Martha stayed on her substitute dose as the years passed. Something had changed in her metabolism since the pregnancy. As the dose shrank the withdrawal became intense. In the old days she would regularly get herself clean but now she was worried that she would be on treatment indefinitely. The urge to use again magnified each time the clinic doctor tried to persuade her to cope on a lower dose. Recovery was the goal and the professionals had targets to meet. Martha began to feel like a victim of the crude clinic system. Talk of rehabilitation, and groups made up of recovering junkies, became a threat rather than the thing she was supposed to be anticipating. To make the withdrawal less uncomfortable Martha started to bring home cans of super-strength lager, for when Billy was in bed, and all Martha had to counter the boredom was the TV. The alcohol dulled her brain in the evenings, and the following mornings.

The only good thing which happened was a council flat where Billy had his own bedroom and there was enough living space. The flat was on the ninth floor and had views across the city. It had a balcony which faced south, adding a sunny disposition. It also brought a host of new problems. Martha had to beg the social services for a loan to buy the basic furniture. She had no idea how to paint or decorate, so the place retained traces of the people who had lived there before. Despite the new environment Martha despaired about the future. She felt trapped in the edifice of her addiction; she had no education and no skills that would persuade someone to employ her; she knew that her ability to look after Billy was limited to angry outbursts when he was disobedient, which was most of the time. And then there were the neighbours. They were noisy, particularly at night, and it took very little time for Martha to recognise the signs of drugs being dealt and used next door. She also knew that it was only a matter of time before she succumbed.

One evening the thumping music and shouting from the neighbours was loud. Martha had started on the lager cans early and emboldened by alcohol she knocked on the door. She knew there was no point in complaining; they would laugh at her. The alternative was to join them. The door was opened by a woman with a familiar face who Martha thought she recognised from the clinic.

'Hello, love' the woman said, 'we been expectin' you'.

There were about half a dozen people sitting around the living room, in various states of consciousness. Martha was drawn effortlessly into the user environment with which she was so familiar. Someone handed her a syringe, already filled. Her craving was overwhelming and without thinking she set about injecting herself. Martha relapsed comprehensively with a ready supply of heroin next door. After the first hit they made her pay for what she used. She re-joined the underclass of petty criminality, from which her pregnancy had rescued her several years ago, and sank hopelessly into the street life she had abandoned since she had become a single mum.

Billy was growing fast. He was tall for his age, wiry and aggressive. He had no sense of discipline, no respect for authority and a smouldering anger and resentment towards the poverty and hopelessness into which he had been born. Martha did not possess the insight to understand his inner rebellion and tried to impose her will on him by shouting at him in angry frustration. Billy ignored her and was intolerant of the incessant harangue. He often left the flat, banging the door behind him, in search of the street life which thrived on the estate. By the time Billy was approaching ten years old he had already lost any fear of authority which might have restrained him. He knew the bad guys, the petty criminals and, of course, the dealers. He stole from shops when he needed to and learnt to sell stuff to kids who had money. He had no real friends but he was accepted by the kids on the streets not least because of his reckless lack of fear of consequences. He did not care what happened to him. Before he was ten years old he had done cannabis, alcohol and a variety of legal highs, all readily available to him on the street for small sums of money. His attendance at the local comprehensive school was sporadic but he had already learnt more on the street than in the class room.

On Billy's tenth birthday Martha hoped he might stay at home with her. She had saved enough to buy him new jeans, a colourful tee-shirt and trendy trainers. Middle class birthday parties with kids and cakes and party-bags were unknown to Billy. As usual Billy was out after school. It was early summer and the streets were still bright during the evening. Martha had used earlier in the day because she did not want Billy to see her injecting herself. She started the third can of the evening, feeling she deserved to celebrate her son's birthday even in his absence. She went to the balcony and craned over the safety bar to see if Billy was in sight. The view to right and left was obscured by the neighbouring balconies. She fetched a chair and climbed on to it to get a better view of the street. The alcohol had made her unsteady. She gripped the safety bar tightly, but her weight was wrongly balanced and she lurched forward over the edge of the balcony. In slow motion she felt herself falling forward, helpless to stop the inexorable slide into the void. She rolled over the safety bar and her weight tore her grip from the bar as she screamed and plummeted from the ninth floor. She hit the pavement, and died instantly, as Billy appeared along the street.

On his tenth birthday Billy became an orphan. He had no idea who his father was and did not care. He always suspected that his mother had killed herself on purpose, and that he was partly to blame, but no one would ever know the truth. Martha's hideous death stayed with Billy for the rest of his life, through the misery of being a 'looked after' child, becoming homeless in his teens and his own descent into drug-taking criminality and violence.

As Billy became acclimatised to his new identity and was encouraged to talk about himself, and listen to the stories of other dispossessed people of his age, he began to understand that they were all telling the same story. Their lives were shaped by the absence of parents, poverty, alienation and the all-pervasive power of opiate dependence and its consequences. They were streetwise, like a feral tribe. None of them had anything to lose.

On his sixteenth birthday Billy was decanted from the protected environment of the orphanage to a hostel for homeless men. He was bemused and angry, barely educated and owned almost nothing. The future was empty of anything he could look forward to. He remained reliant on state benefits as he had done for the whole of his short life, supplemented by the proceeds of petty theft. His only social contact was with men, older than himself, all one step away from destitution, most of whom had drug problems. He started to smoke cannabis every day. In due course he was offered heroin for free. Someone taught him to inject himself and at a stroke opened the door to every kind of harm which opiates cause. The heroin was not free for long but by then Billy was dependent and desperate for a hit. To get enough money to pay for his habit he became a habitual thief, selling stuff on the local fence. In a short space of time Billy's life revolved around the means of obtaining money, scoring, using and repeating the process all over again, day after night after day. The key-workers and social workers were helpless in the face of the overwhelming compulsion of his addiction.

Billy had become an expert. He was an authentic junkie. He knew how to shoplift and learned to nick things from the public when they left their possessions visible. He knew who would give him money for the stolen things. He knew where to find the dealers and exactly what he needed to feed his habit. His life was subsumed to the control of heroin addiction. Consideration for his own safety and well-being was relegated to the urgency of scoring and using. There was no time for anything else. His life followed an ironic pattern; the heroin was not particularly harmful itself but everything associated with it harmed Billy or someone else. He lived outside the law dependent on an illegal drug and committed crimes to obtain it every day. His tolerance of the drug grew as time went by and his habit grew in proportion, and so did the cost. His thieving became more reckless. The meagre benefits, for which he had to sign on at regular intervals, might keep him supplied for a day. He started to borrow money from other users, which he could not repay, and earned himself resentment and then reprisals. In due course he was badly beaten by a bunch of hardened, hostel-dwelling men, to all of whom he owed money. A staff member at the hostel called an ambulance. The first encounter Billy had with judgemental authority was in the A&E department of the hospital.

The green clad ambulance people had been affable enough, and installed Billy on a stretcher in a cubical behind the regulation curtains. He then became subject to the paternalism of the medical profession. He allowed himself to be examined and questioned; there was no reason not to tell his inquisitors honest answers. The doctors told him he would be X-rayed and have his blood tested. He had never heard himself being talked about in his own presence; talked over and discussed, without being included in the conversation. What he heard was only partly comprehensible. What he could understand seemed to be critical and judgemental. His impetuous anger, never far below the surface, spilled over. He sat up, swore at the nurse and doctor, tried to stand up and collapsed on the cubical floor.

They picked him up and helped him back on the couch. The doctor checked him over again, then left. An older nurse in a dark blue uniform came into the cubicle, folded her arms, leant against the couch and looked at him steadily. She took him in like dozens before him, thin, unwashed, long unkempt hair, his left arm bruised and tracked. She spoke to him quietly, addressing him as Billy. 'You've got to let us do what's necessary. We'll get you out as soon as we can. I promise. We've not seen you before have we?' His angry defences fell away. An inch of kindness touched a rarely accessed part of Billy's brain. He was overwhelmed by the pain in his face and ribs where he had been hit and kicked. In due course he had been X-rayed, bled and given some pills for the pain. He was judged fit to leave. The older, kindly nurse gave him a small card with a date written on it. He was to return in a week to get the blood test results.

Billy was clucking. He had to get a hit. The pain from his injuries was made worse by a deeper ache which he knew was withdrawal. By chance he met a man on the street who he knew was a dealer. He had ten pounds left in the world, which his assailants had not found, lodged in the back pocket of his jeans. He stopped the dealer, handed him the tenner, pocketed a small bag of heroin and hurried on to the hostel. He slipped in unnoticed, got to his room, still wrecked after the violence earlier in the day, cooked up and injected. As he sank into an uneasy sleep he knew he would wake in a few hours, desperate for another hit, with no means of obtaining it.

The chaos of Billy's life became worse as his debtors would not leave him alone. Violent encounters became a daily hazard, interrupting his busy pursuit of the next fix. Mostly he sustained minor injuries and learnt to fight back. Occasionally something hurt so badly he took himself back to the hospital to check he had not been badly injured. On each occasion the kindly nurse sought him out, chatted quietly, sometimes teased him about his dreadful appearance, never judged and asked solicitously what was going on his life. Slowly, she started to talk about the possibility of getting help. She did not advise or admonish, simply told him about clinics and one or two local surgeries, which were sympathetic to junkies. Of course Billy had long forgotten about the appointment which he was supposed to attend for his blood test results, so the nurse told him one day that although he had not formally consented to it, the doctors had screened him for all the likely viral infections which he might have contracted through using. They were all negative, so far.

Kindness was painful for Billy. It impinged on some part of his mental sensorium which was raw because it had never been used. So when something touched the part of his brain which needed to respond to it he did not know how and, more than once, found himself in tears in the presence of this unaccustomed assault on his sensibility.

The other thing which Billy had escaped, so far, was the law, although he was known to the police because he was conspicuous by his dishevelled, hard-faced, dead-eyed appearance. He was the epitome of a streetwise user, recognisable for what he was to anyone. Billy knew this and it created a paradoxical ambivalence in his attitude. One part of him wanted to look like what he was, projecting the awfulness of his life to the public, because that somehow validated his miserable existence; another part knew that his life was in the gutter and his self-esteem with it, more pariah than person.

After five years constantly on the run after the next fix, thieving, dodging his creditors and the police, Billy was exhausted and sick of his life. He had made more enemies than friends during his career as a junkie and now he was lonely; he had never had more than a passing relationship with anyone. Help was available but he barely possessed the social skills to ask for it. He found his way to the clinic which was in a part of the city where he went regularly to score and recognised dealers on the pavement outside the clinic. In the reception area a variety of people sat about waiting for something. Billy assumed that he would be seen and somehow helped. After a short exchange with the receptionist he was informed that he would need an appointment for an assessment. The appointment was ten days away. He dropped the appointment card on the counter, left, and scored with the first dealer he met.

This was the first of a series of encounters with people and places where he had been lead to believe that help was available. The system seemed to be designed for some other sort of problem and someone else's convenience. Billy needed help when he asked for it, not next week or the week after. He had never kept an appointment in his life and did not have the time or patience, in the chaotic turmoil of his life, to fit in with someone else's arrangements. An insidious sense of despair engulfed him. Apart from the transient relief of using, there was nothing to look forward to. His life seemed devoid of purpose. For the first time Billy began to think he would be better off dead. Overdosing seemed an obvious way to solve the pointlessness of his existence. He bought a bottle of cheap Vodka and as much heroin as he could afford, locked himself in his hostel room, injected himself with a massive hit, lay on the bed and started to drink the Vodka from the bottle. In due course he passed out.

Billy's state of mind had been noticed by the hostel staff, and when he did not appear for his usual foray after another hit, one of the staff decided to check up on him. Predictably, Billy ended up in the hospital where he was resuscitated. Having hit rock bottom Billy had his first chance to resurrect himself. He was kept on the ward for three days because of his emaciated state. For the first time he was given methadone to stop the withdrawal. No one told him that he would become powerfully addicted to methadone and that getting off methadone was more difficult than stopping heroin. He was discharged from the hospital having had one addiction exchanged for another. He would have to attend the chemist daily where the pharmacist was empowered to watch Billy swallow his daily dose. A new rigmarole imposed itself but criminality, theft and running after the dealers was no longer a part of it.

By trying to end his life Billy had finally attracted attention to himself. He was absorbed into the clinic system. His mental health was scrutinised. He was passed onto the psychologists, who taught him strategies to handle the craving for heroin, which continued to afflict him daily. Later the counsellors gradually got him to start talking about himself. At first this seemed to make things worse as each encounter emphasised the vacuity and pointlessness of his short life, the harm he had done and the hurt to himself; they got him to talk about his street life on the estate, his mum and her death on the pavement at his feet, his time in the kids home with the other dispossessed boys and girls, his slide into drugs. He searched for meaning but found none. Billy's education amounted to little; he could read and write. He discovered that when someone was ready to listen to him he was articulate. His language was colourful and his imagination allowed him to tell the counsellors the finer detail of street life and survival, how to thieve and rapidly dispose of the goods, how the life of a junkie was a full time occupation driven by the destructive power of opiate dependence. In time his experience of his own life reformulated itself into something he started to value, perhaps because of its contemporary awfulness. He started to see himself as a victim, and with that, came a paradoxical power, which gave him a sense of mastery of his dismal past, a glimmer of hope for the future and the idea of self-esteem.

Billy learnt that any hope of recovery depended on distancing himself from other users. In the hostel this was not possible as smack was available to anyone able to pay. He used on a few occasions but did not relapse seriously. One day the social worker found him at the clinic and announced that he had been allocated a small council flat. It was on the fringe of the city far away from the drug infested city centre. Billy had to visit the place and was told he either had to accept the flat or be removed from the housing list. This was his only chance. He agreed. The prescribing of his methadone was transferred to a distant clinic and he was required to go through all the assessment and counselling, which had got him this far, once more. He succumbed to the monotony of keeping himself well and able to function with the regular methadone dosing, which he was allowed to administer himself.

Withdrawal from methadone was a painful and slow process. Each time the clinic reduced his dose the craving became worse. Years passed and Billy resigned himself to indefinite reliance on his daily dose. He started to volunteer to help other users. His expertise was considerable and a little training made him useful enough to the system which conducted the futile war on drugs. He knew well about the trap of poverty, deprivation and submergence into the morass of drug abuse and addiction through which he had come years before. Nothing seemed to have changed. Everyone he tried to help related the same narrative he had told his own counsellors, over and over again.

In time Billy met a woman with whom he had the first functional relationship of his life. He stepped away from his involvement with the drug scene and his life adopted a more prosaic pattern. He understood the depressing reality that the dealers had won. As long as heroin use was illegal there was little hope for the generations trapped in the street culture where addiction thrived. When Billy's partner became pregnant and in due course had a healthy boy, Billy new one thing for certain; as long as he remained alive Martha's grandson would never be a user.

Forty-one

Yesterday I was forty-one years old.

According to my mother I am now 'on the shelf'. This is because I am single with no prospect of a meaningful relationship with either a man or a woman. I have had a number of boyfriends, none of whom were sufficiently empathetic in bed to make me want to spend the rest of my life sleeping with them. Relationships with women remain mysterious to me. Apart from socialising with girlfriends, I do not think I know how they work, and do not feel much desire to find out.

Being on the metaphorical shelf is not necessarily a bad thing. As long as the shelf is not too close to the ground it provides a vantage point from which to survey the scene. Things on shelves have the potential to be taken down to resume their normal function, or even a new one. So I am secretly content with the situation.

I am thin and not very tall. I have short, dark hair and brown eyes. I am pretty, but people do not notice me. I like dressing unimaginatively, so I rarely wear anything other than black tops, (cashmere is my favourite), and black, skinny jeans, every day. This is another thing which my mother believes keeps me confined to the shelf. I like being thin and do not have to make an effort to stay the shape I am, although I like jogging, which probably helps, and also creates a sense of well-being.

Horticulture has been my life and work for longer than I can remember. Years ago I was a landscape designer, shifting earthworks in suburban gardens, but now I spend the day in an office designing the colour and layout of civic flowerbeds on a computer, matching the sophistication of the design to the meagre council budget allocated for the purpose. My plans are emailed to the gardening department and sometimes implemented by the council gardening team. These days I never have to get my hands muddy or freeze in winter gardens. If the weather is fine I sometimes go and inspect the outcome of my designs on quality control visits. I live in a state of constant surprise that my employment continues. It would be easier for the local council to outsource my job. I have thought about setting up a horticultural design company and tendering for the work I do for the council, but general inertia has so far prevented me from taking this radical step.

I live alone in a small, rented flat (without a garden) which I keep obsessively tidy. I like entertaining and have regular evenings of eating and drinking with a handful of close friends, all women. Men, if there were any, would spoil the intimate, gossipy atmosphere of these occasions.

Today is Saturday and I am recovering from the excesses of my birthday party, which I held in the flat with six girlfriends, on Friday evening. My mother, who is nearly eighty and has lived on her own in a modern, expansive bungalow with a colourful garden, since my Dad died ten years ago, has decided to take me out for lunch and then go shopping. My mother is elegant and colourful, like the place she lives in. Because she objects to my chosen style of dressing, she will want to buy me clothes which I shall never wear. She insists that I should do something about what she refers to as my self-esteem, which she considers deficient. I prefer to remain invisible. I am convinced that someone will discover me in due course, but in the meantime I prefer to remain a well-kept secret.

Coping with my mother and a hangover at the same time will be troublesome. Exercise is a panacea for most things and I decide that an hour's jog will be therapeutic. As soon as the weather is clement I put away my winter leggings and insulated running tops and instead wear a pair of small, stream-lined shorts and a skimpy top, all black of course, for my jogging excursions. My feet are clad in pink trainers. It is about as near to running naked as is practically possible and feels physically and mentally liberating, in equal measure. The warmth of the English sunshine on my skin is sensual as I scamper through the parks and suburbs. Running is a solitary activity, a time to reflect and ruminate and watch the passage of the seasons in the suburban parks and gardens. Problems get solved and ideas evolve. For me it has always been like therapy.

After a long shower, and dressed in my regular black, I feel ready to be nagged about my appearance, being single at my age and lack of career prospects. This happens over lunch, and a pleasing bottle of nicely chilled white wine, which helps with my general recovery from the night before. As my mother and I have similar ideas about food we eat elaborate salads and an unctuous chocolate thing for pudding. My mother is genuinely fond of me and has my interests at heart. The problem is that she is, and always has been, everything which I am not. Her elegance, assertiveness and general physical presence create a sort of flamboyance of which I am incapable. I feel diminished in her presence and her hectoring does nothing to inflate my self-esteem, so I have learnt to listen and never argue. Her admonishment is kind but somehow misdirected. It creates a dissonance between us and probably reflects the enduring dynamic in our small family in which my Dad and I had been inseparable since before I can remember; my mother probably felt marginalised, which had never been strictly true.

Having survived lunch I am marched to the local high street in search of expensive clothes which I shall never wear. On this occasion my mother finds me a dress which I actually like. It is made of a soft combination of linen and silk, tight-fitting and short, with a long zip at the back, but most satisfactorily it is black and there is no other colour. I am secretly delighted by the understated style of the dress and hug my mother for her generosity. She dismisses my affectionate behaviour and says something about being colourless and why could I not choose something which would make people notice me, which sums up our dissonant relationship. My birthday celebrations are over. We go our separate ways, still friends.

Whenever I see my mother I wish that my dad was still alive. I was his only daughter and we loved each other with a devoted affection which only happens between Dads and daughters. His too soon death from cancer is still painful ten years on. He was fiercely protective of me and I could do no wrong. His support and encouragement were unwavering and in our small family I was always his pretty little daughter for whom nothing was denied, within reason. The grandiose ambitions which my mother designed for me were systematically diluted and undermined by Dad, unless I agreed with whatever the plan was to be. Inevitably our triangular relationship was fraught with tensions. With hindsight my mother had to be content with watching as her husband and daughter became more and more collusive and introspective about what was best for me. Although I know that she feels the loss of Dad as sadly as me, I suspect she blames him for my failure to make a proper life for myself. Without Dad's protective kindness I feel vulnerable whenever I have to meet my mother.

A week after my birthday I am woken at seven o'clock on Sunday morning by the doorbell. I had been deeply asleep, dreaming about something horticultural to do with stamens, pistils and anthers. It is a recurring dream which I like because of its vaguely Freudian allusions. The only thing to hand with which to cover my nakedness is the little black dress which is still hanging on the wardrobe door knob, with the shop label attached. I struggle into it and go to the front door. Two police women are outside. They ask to come in. Before they start on their practiced explanation I know what they have come to tell me. I am speechless and feel suddenly exhausted. I sit down, bury my face in my hands and sob as one of them gently tells me that my mother has been found dead in her garden early this morning. She must have been doing something in the early sunshine, or perhaps had woken not feeling well and gone out for fresh air.

I had imagined this moment many times. My mother was old but not unwell. The inevitability of her death was something I lived with. The reality is worse than anything I had tried to anticipate.

A helpless loneliness descends like a dense veil. The policewomen drench me with kindness, ply me with coffee and wait while I shower and dress in my customary garb, which is ironically appropriate in the circumstances. They drive me to the mortuary, to where my mother has been removed and where I have to identify her body. The day passes in a haze of formalities to do with post-mortems, advice about how to register her death, pieces of paper, retrieval of the jewellery she had been wearing and who could or should be contacted. Eventually my guardian policewomen take me home, make more coffee and leave me alone.

When my Dad died he had done it slowly, which was not very nice for him, but everyone he left behind had time to accept their imminent loss. I was intimately involved with looking after him in the final stages and we had been able to feel and say a long goodbye. After he was dead I became incapacitated by grief and had to see counsellors and doctors who, although well-meaning, did not seem to have the means to address the infinitely painful separation from the only person in the world who had loved me unconditionally, and whose love I reciprocated. The emotional pain was excruciating and I am still moved to tears by small things which remind me of him. Discovering how to accept the loss is a slow and mysterious journey. My mother had died almost impetuously, without warning, and maybe that is the best way to do it. I am sure she did not suffer. But it is not so good for the people left behind. Because of the way I had felt after Dad's death I suppose I had mentally prepared myself for the sense of grief which would inevitably happen when my mother eventually succumbed. So now that it has happened I feel I know how I should feel, and although it is worse than I had expected, it think it will be easier to cope with, after the initial shock.

Now that I am alone, tears flood down my face and I cannot stop them. I cannot identify clearly what I feel, other than misery. Self-pity seems particularly irrational, but that is what it is, and I hate it. My mother made me feel vulnerable, both alive and dead, and now I have a sense of guilt that her death evokes feelings which I despise. The police women have told me that because my mother's death was sudden the coroner will insist on a post-mortem to find out why she died, which seems pointless. Her death is a fact; I cannot see why knowing the cause will help, unless she was murdered, a thought which I quickly banish. In the meantime I have to contact an undertaker to arrange her funeral, which will be a cremation, after which I suppose her ashes will be scattered with my dad's. I am ambivalent about whether that is what they would want but then I think that when I die I could also be scattered with them and may be that would be a happy reunion. I decide that this is an ordeal which can wait until tomorrow; today is still Sunday anyway, although it seems to have gone on forever.

I do not have the courage to start phoning the girl-friends yet because I know I shall dissolve on the telephone. The weeping becomes less convulsive after a while and I realise that the day-light has begun to fade. I know I need to do something to stem my emotional turmoil and not give in to imminent despair.

Resort to my usual panacea is the obvious solution. I go to the bedroom, undress, pull on my very small, streamlined, black shorts and the skimpy, black top, lace the pink trainers tightly and scamper off into the anonymity of the gathering dusk.

Mabel and Mary

Mabel was ninety-two. There was nothing much wrong with her but age had made her frail. Living so long was all very well but she was not certain if she really wanted to go on indefinitely. The idea of death did not concern her; it was the process of dying which she thought might be tiresome. She decided to spend more time in bed. Her bedroom, in her Georgian terraced house, had always been her favourite place.

The bedroom was on the second floor and over-looked the back garden and the neighbouring row of houses. It had two, tall, South-facing sash windows which made the room bright. The walls were lined with pitch pine panels which gave the room a warm glow. A placid Dutch sea-scape hung on the wall between the windows with a large expanse of pale blue sky. There was a chest of draws made of walnut and an ancient tall boy, which had contained Mabel's mother's possessions decades before. Half the room was filled by Mabel's bed with its huge oak head-board. She slept under a sumptuous duvet covered by acres of white linen.

Every morning the house-keeper arrived at eight o'clock. She made coffee and brought it to the bedroom; she would draw the heavy curtains, flooding the room with day light. In the adjoining bathroom she filled the four-legged Edwardian bath with gallons of steaming water. After the first cup of coffee Mabel arose stiffly from her bed, padded across the soft pile of the green carpet to the bathroom, and clambered into the bath, where she wallowed for half an hour, while the house-keeper changed the bed linen. Glowing from the bath, Mabel returned to the bed, where she luxuriated on a heap of pillows beneath the mountainous duvet, with the coffee on the bedside table, books and the radio, until lunch time. If this was dying, Mabel was content to go on doing it a little longer.

Mabel was not inclined to morbid rumination but dying mattered for a number of reasons. She was determined that it should not be a protracted process; it must happen at home; and like most of her generation, she had an aversion to being a burden on anyone else. The problem was that most of this was not within her immediate control and having to be dependent on other people was unthinkable. Mabel had friends and her devoted house-keeper, but it was more than Mabel could expect that she should ever do more than her usual domestic tasks. She also had a daughter, who lived abroad with her husband who had an overpaid job for an organisation based in South-East Asia. She rarely saw her but letters arrived with filial regularity. Mabel had not mastered email. She would reply cursorily to these dutiful missives, mainly to let her daughter know that she was still alive. Mabel's husband had died suddenly from a heart attack just before his eightieth birthday, ten years ago. It was typical of her husband to have a convenient death, causing no trouble to anyone, but leaving a yawning void in his widow's life. She needed a way to gain control over her dying; she needed a strategy.

Mabel was hesitant to discuss this subject with the friends whom she met two or three times a week, at the local patisserie, for cakes and coffee. They would be sure to misconstrue her intention and think she had a fiendish plan to end her life. She was at a loss to know to whom she could turn for advice about how to die. Thinking that maybe it was something doctors could help with, she booked an appointment with her GP. Having always been in good health Mabel was not familiar with the surgery and did not really know her doctor.

The afternoon of the appointment arrived. Mabel had ordered a taxi to take her the short distance to the surgery. She arrived punctually and was irritated to be kept waiting for twenty minutes. In due course she was ushered into the presence of the doctor. What could he do for her? Mabel felt instantly patronised. She explained that she was seeking advice about dying, not death, which did not pose a problem. How could she ensure that her death should happen at home, that it was rapid and did not cause a tedious problem to other people? To his credit the doctor listened patiently, refraining from interrupting until Mabel had explained her dilemma. He proceeded to ask a series of questions, which, he explained, were to clarify the situation. Mabel had the impression that the doctor suspected that she was a little unhinged, such was the nature of his enquiries, concerning her mood, daily habits and source of enjoyment in life. He offered to help her complete a form, which would serve as a directive, in the event that Mabel should ever lose the capacity to determine her own affairs. She agreed to do this more to please the doctor than because she felt it provided a solution. What she really wanted was something of a more practical nature, but neither she nor the doctor seemed able to identify exactly what that might be. She returned home with a sense of exasperation.

A few days later Mabel was surprised to be telephoned by a woman, with a youthful voice, who introduced herself as a community psychiatric nurse, called Mary. Mabel's doctor had asked her to get in touch. He had expressed concern that Mabel may be depressed and was contemplating doing herself harm. Would it be alright for her to call in and see her? No, said Mabel, it would not be alright. She had never been depressed and had no intention of being so now. Neither did she have any intention of harming herself and would not know how if she wanted to, unless staying in bed until lunchtime was considered risky behaviour. In her youthful voice Mary became more insistent. She thought it would be sensible for her to come round and have a chat, particularly in view of the conversation which Mabel had had with her doctor.

The sense of exasperation which Mabel had felt after her appointment re-asserted itself. She had the distinct feeling of being put under surveillance. As it was not a patisserie afternoon Mabel reluctantly agreed to see Mary the following day, but not before three o'clock. Mary arrived punctually at the appointed time. She was not very tall, neatly dressed in the contemporary uniform of tight jeans, tee-shirt and flat shoes. Her hair was dark and cut short, like a boy. She had lots of piercings in her ear-lobes and one side of her nose. Her eyes were brown, her nose straight and her mouth was small which somehow made her voice even more youthful than it had sounded on the telephone. Mabel thought she could not be much more than twenty years old. To her surprise she took an instant liking to her; she looked vulnerable.

Mabel took Mary to the kitchen, which was spotless after the house-keeper's ministrations during the morning. She sat Mary at the ancient, oak table and wandered about gathering a tin of unctuous looking Belgian biscuits and making tea in a pot, a process unfamiliar to Mary who belonged to a tea-bag generation.

'Now, my dear,' said Mabel, 'what can I do for you?' She deliberately mimicked the manner of her doctor, wondering if Mary felt patronised. She sat down opposite Mary and looked at her steadily.

'What exactly is a community psychiatric nurse?' Mabel asked before Mary could respond to her initial enquiry. Mary explained in her girl's voice that she looked after people with mental health problems, not in the hospital but in their homes.

'Well,' said Mabel, 'that sounds very well-meaning but as I don't have a mental health problem perhaps you would like to tell me about yourself?' Mary was used to verbal obstruction and if talking to Mabel about herself was going to allow her to make some sort of connection she was happy to go along with it.

She started on a potted history of how she had become involved with mental health. Mary grew up in North London and went to the local comprehensive. She was bright and got to University in Newcastle. In her final year she had become depressed and made a half-hearted attempt to kill herself. She had been admitted to a mental hospital briefly and gained all sorts of insights into the working of the mental health services. Rather than putting her off, the experience of being a patient had made her decide that working in mental health would be an interesting career. The depression got better, although she felt she would never quite be rid of the emotional vulnerability which the episode had left her with. She had to do a great deal more post-graduate training to become what she was now. She was twenty-eight and felt she knew her job well and that actually, having had a mental illness, and seen the psychiatric services as a patient, she thought she was able to relate to her clients more empathetically.

Mabel was a good listener and allowed Mary to finish her story. 'My dear,' she said, 'you have had a very hard time. What about your people, your family?' She asked, in her patrician tones.

'All dead,' replied Mary. 'My mum and dad died in a car accident in France three years ago. Now,' said Mary, 'what about you?'

'Oh, my dear,' sighed Mabel, 'your short life has been much more difficult than mine. I went to University in London, then Paris, decades ago. I met a nice man in the diplomatic service and we got married. We lived in South America, South East Asia and half a dozen European capitals. It was a marvellous life. Always meeting new people; I had to learn to interview them by way of conversation, because we always had to be talking to them, even if they did not speak English. And are you on your own or do you have a young man to look after you? You look so young.'

'No,' said Mary, looking away, 'no young man in my life.' Mabel knew she had been hurt, the sudden loss of eye contact, which had been constant, silently spoke of sadness.

Mabel knew about loss. 'You do look sad all of a sudden. Were you hurt very badly?' Mary realised the conversation had overstepped a boundary; she was being interviewed.

'Let's not talk about that now. We are supposed to be talking about you.'

'Ah, my dear,' said Mabel, 'you should know, I never talk about myself. I do love hearing about other people and it is most enjoyable talking to you, in particular. So you had to get rid of your young man,' she added perspicaciously, 'I have a sense that it was all rather unpleasant.'

'Yes,' Mary gave up. 'Yes, you're right; I've had a difficult time, quite emotional. But it's over now.' Mabel leant across the table and quite spontaneously took Mary's hand in hers.

'But are you really over it?' Mary dissolved, overwhelmed by Mabel's tide of kindness. 'I can see you need consoling and we both need more tea.' She got up from the table and put the kettle on again. She plonked a box of tissues on the table for Mary.

The tea ritual complete, Mabel sat down and poured, using a silver strainer to keep the leaves from the cups. A short interval, and a tissue with which to veil her emotional turmoil, was enough to allow Mary to regain her composure.

'I'm so embarrassed,' said Mary in a small voice. 'I came here to look after you and now look at me.' She giggled haltingly, the tears still just beneath the surface.

'My dear, you are a very charming young woman. It is seldom that I find I can instantly like people. There is something about you that makes me want to look after *you*. I'm afraid I can't help it. So please forget about me, I'm not barmy or depressed, and tell me what has made you so wretched.'

Mary gazed out of the kitchen window at the paved garden and the red brick of the garden wall. She was used to being supervised and helped to handle the emotional provocation intrinsic to her work, but the warm sincerity of Mabel's spontaneous kindness overwhelmed her. Her carefully rehearsed professional boundaries evaporated.

'It wasn't a man,' Mary explained slowly. 'There never has been a man. I'm gay. My girlfriend decided to finish our relationship two weeks ago. It all came as a surprise and I've been very upset. I still love her.'

Mabel was not easily discomfited but she realised that she had been insensitive. Her usually sharp antennae had failed. It dawned on her that her sudden liking for Mary was something to do with her sexuality; her gamine boyishness, her small frame, short hair, piercings in her ears and the youthful voice touched something atavistic in Mabel's long experience. Mabel smiled at her. Long ago she had longed for a son; there had been no more babies after her daughter had been born. Mary had come to look after her but now all that Mabel could think of was how to comfort this vulnerable, half-girl, half-boy.

'Poor you,' said Mabel. 'Had you been together for long?'

'Ages,' replied Mary. 'We're the same age and we started to live together when we were both twenty-five. I thought it was going to be for life. But she woke the other morning and told me she didn't love me anymore and was going to leave. I didn't believe her at first. She was calm and kind about it but said there was no use pretending. She packed her stuff and left. I think she's with her mum now. That's what I could do with just now – a Mum. Oh dear, this is all very unprofessional.'

'Mary, my dear, never mind about being professional. This will all get worse before it gets better. You can't expect to get over this sort of thing in a trice. You need a Mum and I have a great deal to offer. I can't be your mother but I can be something like one. Now, I'm sure you have more people to rescue from their follies this afternoon, but if you have time later I should love to cook you a consoling supper.'

Mary studied the table top fighting back the tears again. She was disarmed by Mabel's kindness. 'I'd love to,' she said. 'I am afraid I'm a veggie, but I could bring something back if it helps.'

Mary hastened off to look after her clients in the community and Mabel donned her apron in preparation to feed her new child, of whom she was unaccountably fond, and drench her with kindness. She cooked a ratatouille, soaked lentils in preparation for a dhal, found a heap of new potatoes in the cupboard and frozen spinach and broad beans in the freezer, which she could turn into something. By the time Mary came back, armed with a large granary loaf, the kitchen table was covered in bowls of healthy looking food. Mabel handed Mary a bottle of white Burgundy from the fridge and pointed her to a drawer where she kept the corkscrew.

They took the wine through to the drawing room, which adjoined the kitchen, through tall pine doors. The room was elegant, book-lined, sumptuously furnished, deeply carpeted and with a large fire-place. They sat opposite each other on luxurious sofas on either side of the hearth. How were the clients this afternoon? Enquired Mabel. Mary did not want to talk about her work so replied that nothing unusual had happened. She added that she would have to report something about Mabel to her manager. Mabel suggested that she did not feel that she appeared to present a risk, so her case could be closed. Mary thought that this approach was not too far from the truth. Mabel really wanted to know about Mary. She had no experience of gay women, or their relationships, and was anxious to find out about Mary's life. Was she happy being gay?

'Of course,' said Mary, 'it's all I've ever known. It started in school with crushes on older girls and teachers. At university it was accepted as a way of life. It was normal, just like gay men. My partner, Emma, and I met at Uni. She was amazing when I got depressed. She just accepted it and helped tremendously with getting me to believe that I would get better. We came back to London at the same time and got together seriously soon after. She's a teacher. We had a really solid relationship and we were in love. My problem is that I still am. We're very alike. We have the same spontaneous thoughts about things. We even look the same. At Uni we were known as the gay twins. For years we did everything together; live, eat, sleep, exercise, shared our clothes. Apart from work hours we were inseparable. At present I really can't imagine living the rest of my life without her. I suppose I'm hanging on to the belief that she may come back but it has to be her decision. At least she texts and phones to check up on me. She knows I'm fragile since the depression. I know it's wrong to put pressure on her but I find it hard not to beg her to come home every time we speak. I guess she needs time if there's a possibility that things can go back to normal.'

'Dear me,' reflected Mabel. 'I'm sure she needs time and you'll need to be very patient. But don't imagine that things can be normal again. There may be a new normality in due course. Once these things have happened life can't be the same as before; it's like bereavement. People don't get over it; they learn to accept it and find new ways to cope. And that's what you must be prepared to do. Does Emma tell you what it feels like for her or are your conversations all about you?'

'So far, all about me. I suppose she feels guilty about hurting me and needs to be sure I'm not going to jump off a bridge or something. She knows how I react to things better than I do myself.'

Mabel looked steadily at Mary, as if she was about to admonish her.

'Never stop telling her that you love her. It matters more than anything else. Such a devoted relationship doesn't die overnight. Emma's affection may have needed a little respite but you can be sure her feelings for you are deep and in time she will return, full of remorse. But I think you must find out how she's feeling, because even if she has a listening family, the only person to whom she can explain what she's really feeling, is you. But don't ask her why she suddenly thought her love for you had dried up. She won't know. Feelings are fickle. However contrary, feelings must be listened to, accepted and nurtured. She's been impetuous and probably does not know how to come back to you, so you need to make it as easy as possible. Now, let's go and eat something. Bring the bottle into the kitchen.'

Mabel stood up stiffly from the low sofa. Mary reached across to help her and Mabel took her arm and allowed herself to be led to the kitchen table. 'Thank you my dear,' said Mabel. 'Now just reach behind you and gather some knives and forks and things from the drawer. And we better have some plates from the dresser.'

They chatted on over the meal. Despite her reservations about talking about herself, Mabel was a practised raconteur and related stories about her life as a diplomatic wife and having to deal with servants in foreign countries. It was a world unknown to Mary who listened enraptured by the colourful stories of life in the steaming tropics and sophisticated Europe.

The meal was over and they washed up together because it was a companionable thing to do. They sat down at the table again with the remains of the bottle.

'Now, Mary,' said Mabel taking charge of the conversation, 'what are you going to do next, about Emma, I mean?'

Mary thought for a minute. 'We've not seen each other since Emma left. I think we should meet.'

Mabel smiled. 'Of course you should; but not at your flat. You must find some neutral ground where Emma feels comfortable. I'm sure you're right; whatever else she may be feeling she'll need a way to deal with her feelings of guilt.'

There they left the subject of Emma. Next time Emma called, Mary would ask her if she wanted to meet. And Mabel wanted to know when she and Mary would meet again. Mary hesitated unsure how to handle Mabel's attention.

'You've been so kind. I really don't want to impose,' she said. 'It's been lovely talking to you. And thank you for your wisdom. It really does help.'

'Let me know when you have arranged to see Emma. Come and see me again after you've met. I want to look after you, whether you like it or not. I shall be insistent. You had better give me your telephone number. You'll have to put up with more than one person checking up on you.' Unwittingly Mary had done what she originally came to do; she had become a new reason for Mabel to stay alive. Mabel could forget about her dying plans.

They hugged briefly on the doorstep as Mary departed. She hurried into the darkening night, smiling at the recollection of Mabel's colonial stories, as tears streamed down her face. She had never been so graciously entertained by someone three times her age. She was overcome by conflicted feelings; moved by Mabel's guileless kindness but miserable at the thought of her absent lover.

Her phone vibrated in the pocket of her jeans. She grabbed it, glancing at the screen to check the name of the caller.

'Emma,' she said, 'I love you. Please can we meet?'

They met on an anonymous park bench, the following day. As Mabel predicted, Emma was full of remorse. She did not know why she had suddenly felt the way she did. They agreed that things did not need to be the same as before; they could do things differently if it helped, just as long as they were still in love, and they agreed that they were.

Emma came back to the flat the day after the meeting on the park bench. In the evening they decided to go out somewhere but Mary had pre-empted the need to decide where.

'Emma' she said, 'I want you to come and meet a new friend.'

Laila and Sophie

In the corner of the room, next to a table laden with wine bottles, a girl in a short, tartan kilt talked rapidly, her small, pretty mouth scattering words around the girl she was talking to, who listened intently. The large, brown eyes of the attentive girl were fixed on her companion's face; her head and neck were enclosed in a tightly wound, pale blue hijab, which perfectly covered her hair, leaving the oval, flawless complexion of her face visible. The end of the fabric was draped elegantly over her shoulder. The rest of her long body was covered by a plain, pale blue kameez; only her face and hands were visible. Her cultural modesty was decidedly fashionable. Both girls had pale café-au-lait skin. The girl in the kilt had long, glossy, black hair and the same large, middle-Eastern eyes as her attentive listener. Her legs were shapely, in opaque black tights. Above the neat kilt she wore a crisp, white shirt, casually unbuttoned at the top.

Drawing closer, in search of a drink from the table next to the girls, I could not resist the temptation to eavesdrop. I proffered the bottle to the kilted girl, who was drinking red wine. She held out her glass, talking ceaselessly. Her companion was not drinking.

'… and his father didn't allow me to enter their house until after we were married. Can you believe it? They were weird. They invited my family but I was excluded. We had to have three ceremonies to get married; civil, religious and social. Almost as soon as we were official my husband started to make rules about the role of the wife in his Muslim family. It really took me by surprise. I thought we were liberal, but no; he decided he was going to exert his cultural origin and I'm sure his family were behind it. They even wanted me to cover up, like you, and I had to when I was finally allowed into his parents' house. They wouldn't even speak to me. I became so angry; I knew I couldn't stay in this relationship. One morning I woke up and looked at him and realised I didn't love him. I wondered if I ever had. I couldn't face him touching me. I got out of the bed and never got back in. So after six months I left and went back to my parents and now we're divorcing. He's being difficult but I don't care. I own nothing anyway, apart from clothes. But I have a job so I don't need his money. And my parents are being really sympathetic, bless them.'

She stopped talking abruptly, wound her fingers in her shiny hair which lay on her right shoulder, and looked at me unsmilingly. Her companion turned towards me and I was surveyed by four huge, brown eyes. I was uncertain if I was meant to have heard the end of their conversation but I was not going to pretend that I had not.

'There's only one cause of divorce,' I suggested.

'Yes?' asked the kilted girl, 'and I can tell, you're going to tell us.'

'Marriage,' I announced. They both smiled, rather unenthusiastically.

'You sound as if you know all about it.'

'Long ago I managed to stay married for ten years before my wife decided she had had enough and left me for someone more entertaining. I've been single ever since. It's hard work staying together; it should not be underestimated. Everything matters from who does the washing up to who initiates sex. Get it wrong enough times and you plant the seed of division. I suspect it's easier to work at relationships when you're not married. There's more at stake. And consent matters so much. No one should believe that they can make rules for someone else.'

The girl with the hijab giggled. 'You're so lucky, Laila,' she looked at her kilted friend. 'If I left my husband I think his family would kill me. He hits me if he thinks I'm out of line. I'm only allowed out with girlfriends. If he hears I've spoken to a man I get beaten. I'm covered in bruises under this.' She tugged at her kameez. 'On my chest and my bum and legs. Once he tried to strangle me. I had to stay at home until the bruises faded. Oh dear,' she looked at me, 'I'm talking to a man. I'm in trouble.' She smiled a sad smile. Laila took her hand. 'Don't be silly, Sophie. D'you want to leave him?'

'Of course I want to leave him. He wants kids but I never will, not while the beating goes on. I told the doctor about him and said I needed a way not to get pregnant, because he wants sex all the time, so my doctor put this coil thing inside me. My husband doesn't know. The doctor wanted me to go to the police but his family are too much trouble if I do anything.'

Laila took her hand in both of her own. She looked at her earnestly.

'Sophie, come and live with me.'

I suppose I knew that these relationships existed but had never heard girls talking candidly to each other about this sort of medieval entrapment. She described a painful vignette of domestic tyranny which seemed to be sanctioned by her community. The awfulness of Sophie's life was alarming. Clearly she did not accept that this had to be her lot in life, but escape seemed elusive.

'Why did you marry him?' I asked naively.

'Family, of course. He's my cousin. We had more or less grown up together. After school he got a job and I went to Uni. Before we got married it seemed OK. It wasn't until after the wedding that everything got difficult. But there's nowhere to go, unless it's the police, and that doesn't always help. Or even if it does, it has bad consequences'.

'Come and live with me,' repeated Laila. 'We can get you a job. I know people who need good Muslim girls to work for them. You have a degree and all that'.

'But we would both be bad Muslim girls. Leaving husbands; living secretly. No one would look at me.'

'Maybe not in the Muslim community but in the secular world of work you wouldn't have a problem,' I suggested.

'You don't understand. Laila's OK. Her family are properly liberal. But I'd be cut off by my family. It's a big stigma. I'd be disowned and they take reprisals, if they can. I know girls who've been through it, spat at, ostracised, denied their own religion even.' Her face looked grave and tears welled in her eyes. Laila put her arms round her. 'Don't, Sophie. You *are* coming to live with me; we can handle it together.' Sophie blotted her tears with the loose end of the hijab and smiled shyly. She looked at me:

'You're not supposed to see all this rubbish. I don't even know who you are.'

'Jeremy,' I said. 'I work as an academic at a university, teaching, researching; that sort of thing. I know this has nothing to do with me; I'm not part of your culture. But ordinary respect for women has to be a way of life, no matter what religion or community you come from. I haven't heard a story like yours before first hand, it sounds brutal and abusive. It's not my business but I think you should leave your husband. If you want a job I can help you get one where I work. Not an academic one, but something which would lead somewhere.' The party had become loud. The drinks had made the guests voluble and disinhibited. It made our tense conversation feel out of place.

‘Please let me give you my name and contacts. Laila had better have it and if you move on and want help, let me know.’

I scribbled a phone number and email on a piece of paper and gave it to Sophie who handed it to Laila.

‘If he finds that he’ll kill me’.

She smiled and seemed to have recovered her composure. I felt suddenly optimistic that some good would come from our encounter and wandered off to see what other company was present. I was angry that such misery could be just beneath the surface in this raucous environment. There was a gulf of unawareness between the oblivious, boozing party-goers and the silent suffering of Sophie’s plight.

Two weeks passed before Laila contacted me by email. Sophie had left her husband. She was living in Laila’s parents’ house where they shared a bedroom. Had I been serious about finding a job for Sophie? Her CV was attached. It was dazzling; a list of ‘A’ levels and a first class degree in sociology, from a university in the Midlands, along with all the usual undergraduate involvement with worthy, student societies. And then it stopped, as if life had ceased on graduation. I assumed that was when she had married and ceased to live her own life. My department was seeking a new receptionist, who would also have a role as PA to some of the academic staff. I forwarded the CV to the recruitment panel with an authoritative recommendation. Sophie got the job. I knew she would excel because graduates working in jobs below their ability always had plenty of initiative and forged a place for themselves, although being an omniscient receptionist was a much more difficult job than was usually recognised.

From time to time I sought out Sophie at work to find out about life when she was not at work. Laila’s parents had been completely supportive. She loved living with

Laila and they shared everything. They were looking for a flat to move to which was affordable with their two salaries. She had been cut off by her own parents; 'you are no longer my daughter' she had been told by her father. Her husband and his family had stayed completely silent, as if she had never existed. Her main anxiety was to keep her new life secret from spies, whom she was sure would be looking for her. Having become involved, I felt a responsibility for her and made it clear that she must let me know if anyone caused her trouble. I had an ominous foreboding that, sooner or later, she would be tracked down and someone would try to harm her.

I felt that socialising with the girls was not appropriate. But every few weeks I was summoned to the new flat for curry. The girl's circle of friends was limited. They trusted few people with their address for fear of intrusion by Sophie's estranged family. They seemed happy and settled, living like sisters. Laila had a new job with a TV channel, doing research work for documentaries, which took her away from the flat at intervals for a few days at a time. Sophie had requested more involvement with the academic activities of the department and, I knew, was well respected in her role by her colleagues. But she retained an aura of sadness. She was still trapped in an impossible marriage, from which there was little prospect of escape. She denied herself male company at home; at work she joined in the banter with everyone, irrespective of gender. She stayed resolutely covered from head to foot, modest and elegant. At home she allowed herself to wear jeans, but kept her hair from view on every occasion when I visited. My concern for her prompted regular enquiries about unwanted contact. She was discrete about her personal life, apart from allowing me in the flat. I made her reinforce her promise that she was to let me know if there was any hint of trouble.

My premonition that they would be found out in due course continued to nag. It became horribly real one morning with a panic phone call from Laila. She was in the North of England for her work. Sophie was in hospital. She had been attacked. I found her on the ward, where Laila had directed me. There was a policeman by her bed. She was still considered to be at risk from her assailant, who had not been caught.

She had been standing at a bus stop when someone had approached her and slashed her face with a razor. A long line of tiny stitches stretched from her left eye to the corner of her mouth. The cut was criss-crossed with narrow strips of adhesive. A nurse interrupted my attempt to discover more of what happened because Sophie had been told to keep her face still to give the wound the best chance of healing. I wanted to know, most of all, if Sophie had recognised her attacker. She shook her head. The policeman spoke for Sophie. There were witnesses; he would certainly be arrested soon. Had Sophie been watched? Did the attacker know her address? The policeman seemed to know some background to Sophie's life, but said he was not at liberty to talk about where the police enquiries were leading. There was little I could do. Laila would return before Sophie was discharged. She was safe enough on the ward. I insisted she must let me know everything that happened; phone, text, email; whatever was available. I went back to work and waited to be contacted.

The plastic surgeon discharged Sophie the following day with instructions to have the stitches removed in five days' time. She was to see the skin specialist in four weeks to check she had healed and be prescribed a camouflage cream, to match her skin colour, which she could use on the scar if she needed it. Laila called me when they arrived at the flat. 'Come round,' she said, 'now!'

I arrived at the flat. Laila opened the door and excitedly dragged me in to see Sophie. Lying on the sofa in the cramped living room she had undergone a sort of transformation. She wore a bright, stripy top and skinny jeans. Dark tresses of her hair tumbled freely over her shoulders; she was beautiful. During her stay on the ward she had reflected long and sadly about her husband and family. She knew the attack was not by chance. There had been no motive; no attempt to steal anything. She was sure it had been a malicious attack on behalf of those who believed themselves to have been insulted by her rebellion. She had decided to rebel more completely. 'I don't think you can stop being a Muslim, but I'm finished with religion and all the stuff that goes with it,' she announced. 'I'm an apostate'. Laila danced round the room waving her arms in the air. 'Freedom!' she shouted and dived onto the sofa to hug her friend.

There remained the sinister possibility that there would be more reprisals. The police had shared the view that the attack had been religiously motivated and took it seriously. The attacker was duly identified, arrested, charged and threatened with a long sentence. He agreed to help the police in return for a more moderate sentence. The evidence had led back to Sophie's husband. The girls were visited by the police a few weeks later. Her husband had not been charged with anything but had been persuaded that in the event of another attempt to harm Sophie, he would be immediately implicated. The lawyers insisted he must grant Sophie a divorce and, in due course, this was achieved. The girls moved to a different part of town as they no longer felt safe in the flat. Sophie found she could not cope with going out alone, so Laila became her constant chaperone.

At work Sophie's transformation was celebrated and admired. The background to the reason for the attack had had to be shared. The staff were appalled by the litany of cruel events in Sophie's life and created a rota to escort Sophie out at lunchtime and someone always walked her home if Laila was busy. She began to feel safer and the novelty of her secular self gave her a new confidence and freedom.

As time went by life became more normal. Laila and Sophie were successful young women. In company they were intelligent and funny. Everywhere they went, still mostly together, they looked formidable, glossy and attractive. To predatory men they were intimidating. By now they were in their late twenties; it was inevitable that one by one they would let men back into their lives. They were discerning and cautious. Past abuses had left deep impressions in their shared narratives. The standards they expected from prospective boyfriends were exacting. From time to time both women found kind and considerate men who respected them as equals or better, but trusting those who wanted to possess them was always an obstacle.

They continued to invite me to their curry evenings, sometimes to discreetly approve of a new companion for one or other of them. Having become deeply attached to these inseparable friends I cared a great deal for their welfare, knowing what had gone before. I watched over them from a safe distance, careful not to intrude. It was impossible not to admire and respect the way in which they had risen above adversity and been faithful and devoted to each other over the years. I began to wonder how they would cope with the prospect of separation from each other, as the boy-friends enticed them into greater intimacy and independence. One day they told me that they had promised each other that they would never marry again. There would be no ceremonies or empty wedding avowals. What they required of their partners was trust and respect. Love also helped. When these ingredients were in sufficient supply they would loosen their mutual bond and try to live without each other. I had no doubt that their friendship would endure, come what may, but the adhesive, which created their attachment for each other, would have to dissolve a little to allow them to make new lives.

Their evolving lives followed a synchronous pattern. While they both found men whom they thought they could love, neither would ever quite trust the opposite sex. Their oppressive marriages cast lugubrious shadows over all their attempts to abandon themselves to guileless relationships. They had a constant insecurity about allowing themselves to be absorbed by the intimacy their partners tried to offer. Reassurance came from each other, but the courage to devote themselves to the sort of commitment their partners sought was elusive. They stayed resolutely unmarried. They joined organisations which campaigned against the oppression of women. When they were together they continued to intimidate men. Then they both got pregnant, almost simultaneously, but not intentionally.

The possibility of another generation of themselves was intoxicating. It was the catalyst which threw them back together. They took their pregnancies home and grew together more inseparably than ever. The men were shut out and they realised that they were a family intact, together; there was no need for anyone else.

Martina and John

Martina believed that she was lucky. Her contentment with life provided the reason for her conviction. She enjoyed being alone. Her independence set her apart from the society which she might have kept; her own company made her happy. On days when she was not able to avoid seeing other people she looked forward to being alone again soon. Often it was hard to avoid company because people sought her out; Martina was pretty in a boyish way. Her hair was short, wavy and unmanageable; her face was made attractive by the fullness of her lips; she liked to dress in layers of knitted clothing and copious shirts, which hung on her slim frame, understating the desirability of her body.

At twenty-eight Martina was happily single. She did not have a family. Her parents had died in the preceding years and she had been their only daughter. Although her family had not been rich, Martina had been left with enough money to allow her to lead her life without having to work for a living, although she did work. She had a number of girlfriends with whom she socialised from time to time. But a boyfriend, a lover, would spoil her contented solitariness. So she lived alone in a small, shiny flat in North London, furnished with modern, minimalist furniture.

Her job was another reason why she thought herself lucky; not because she was employed but because the job allowed her to spend most of the day alone. At university

Martina had read the history of art and obtained a first class degree. Later she had become a specialist in contemporary figurative painters. The degree had been a passport to her job in a gallery near Piccadilly, which sold pictures by modern artists for eye-watering prices. Martina sat all day on a tall chair at the back of the gallery behind a small desk, with a computer on it, in decorative isolation, waiting for occasional customers. The gallery was brightly lit. It had spotless white walls on which hung a few large canvasses at carefully arranged intervals. An empty expanse of shiny, wooden floor filled the space between Martina and the front of the gallery, where an enormous pane of glass separated the peaceful stillness of the gallery from the pavement outside and passing cars in the narrow street. The owner of the gallery had wanted Martina to dress in a style to suit the ambience of his chic West End gallery. She had exchanged her knitted drapery for loose-fitting, diaphanous, silky tops, in muted shades of pink or grey, which flattered her small-breasted figure.

Martina was required to spend many hours every day monitoring the prices of pictures, being sold at auctions around the world, and inform her employer about movements in the market which might be of interest to him. This activity was occasionally punctuated by the entrance to the gallery of people interested in what was hanging on the walls. These were mainly tourists who Martina observed while they wandered around and eventually left. She had learnt to recognise the dealers, who always came alone. She would slide off her tall chair, behind the computer, and walk slowly towards the visitor, stopping at a cautious distance, careful not to intrude, but available for enquiries if the dealer was sufficiently interested. The enquiries were usually about the price, rather than the provenance, of the pictures. Martina knew all the prices of the pictures by heart but made an elaborate charade of consulting the computer, with the object of creating an atmosphere of professional integrity, before quoting an extravagant figure.

Another intrusion on Martina's pleasantly solitary days was the duty to accompany her employer to auctions at fashionable art sales in the West End of London. She was uncertain of her role on these occasions. All the dealers were accompanied by young and attractive women whose main function seemed to be to look decorative, while the dealers exchanged hundreds of thousands of pounds for works of art, which would reappear on the market as soon as the inflated prices inflated some more.

Martina loved her placid life. The pace of events was pleasing, punctuated only by the bustle and excitement of auction days. She was constantly surrounded by beautiful things; the few people with whom she had to associate regarded her with the deference due to the guardian of the gallery. Her employer seemed pleased with the way in which Martina handled the occasional sales from the gallery, and also the reticent style in which she presented the mystery and sophistication of the elegant shop front to the enquiring public.

Although Martina had acquired an extensive knowledge of her chosen niche of figurative art, there remained a great deal to learn. The possibilities for study seemed infinite; the market and emerging artists created a constantly changing landscape which Martina spent many contented hours observing in the quietness of the gallery. From time to time she would encounter an artist worthy of drawing to the attention of her employer. Occasionally, and after long perusal, Martina would be despatched to visit these artists in their studios. The object of the visits was to assess the marketability of the work in progress. Why some were selected, and not others, was beyond Martina's intuition or experience but she willingly embarked on these occasional forays, always alone and armed with a file of information gleaned from her research.

Her visits were met by a combination of cautious welcome, in case she was a potential source of income, and cynicism, as she represented the market place and commodification. Martina was amused and entertained by the idiosyncratic personalities she met. They all had in common talent, in varying measure, and unconditional devotion to their art. She respected and admired them all and knew she must learn to cultivate a relationship with each new potential client if the possible rewards were to be realised. There was a need for trust, a sharing of the understanding of what each could offer the other and ultimately a need to find a way to like each other, which was not always easy as Martina found there was rarely much she had in common with her new protégés.

The pictures were mainly figurative, this being Martina's area of expertise, all necessitating models. Perhaps not surprisingly Martina had many offers to be a subject, all of which she declined as professionally as she could until she encountered an artist who drew fine pencil portraits in a reductionist style, using simple lines with an almost trigonometric approach. The studio in which the artist worked seemed to mimic his style. It was spotless and obsessionally tidy. Everything seemed to be in its own place. It was brightly lit, high ceilinged with a few pieces of furniture standing on the bare, wooden floor. Because she liked his work she allowed herself the indulgence of being drawn. The artist asked to draw her profile. She sat on a plain wooden chair in the middle of the studio while he adjusted the lighting. 'Now, close your eyes, please,' he said. Martina obliged. In a short space of time the portrait was done. It was a finely accurate representation, perfect in its simplicity. Her head was bent slightly forward, her eyelids and lashes minutely drawn. Her nose, which was a little too large for the other proportions of her face, was exact, as was the fullness of her mouth and lips which made her face remarkable and attractive. Her unruly, short hair was pencilled in silhouette. Nowhere had the artist used shading. Martina knew better than to ask to take it with her. She was promised that if she made the artist famous the portrait would be hers, but not before. She smiled, thanked him and left. She would tell her employer that she had found a remarkable talent.

Martina had to acknowledge to herself that it was not just the drawing she liked. The artist had been attentive, polite and seemed genuinely appreciative of Martina's interest in his work. From her research she knew that he made a living from drawing and painting portraits through private commissions but his work was barely known to the public. He was a little older than Martina. He dressed tidily in unassuming clothes. He had a kind face, made kinder when he smiled, which he did a lot, peering over his rimless spectacles. He was clean shaven with receding, sandy hair. She thought she must contrive to visit him again but she would have to do it with the approval of her employer as she would need to close the gallery for an hour or two.

On the pretext of needing to see some of the artist's work a second time Martina arranged another visit. The artist, whose name was John, was delighted that he had made a favourable impression and welcomed Martina, clearly ready to entertain as well as to provide access to his portfolio. Martina remained resolutely professional in her approach. She was determined that nothing in her manner should betray that the reason for her visit was as much to do with her interest in the personal qualities of the artist as the quality of his work. But she needed to know if she had aroused more than professional interest about herself in John. Martina spent a long time looking at the pictures which John presented to her, which persuaded her, that whatever else may be going on, that she had discovered a remarkable talent. She was in no doubt that she would have something worthwhile to report to her employer. John eventually exhausted the succession of pictures which he wanted Martina to view. They were a selection of drawings and oils of portraits and figures of men and women in various stages of undress. She turned to look around the bright, empty space in the studio. Pinned to a small easel on a table, placed discreetly in the corner of the studio, Martina saw the portrait of herself.

Martina hesitated, unsure of the significance of the way the portrait had been displayed. John had obviously meant her to see it but not in the same way that he had wanted her to see the other pictures which he had shown her. He smiled and said 'I think you deserve a frame.' Martina smiled back, pleased by the subtle flirtation. She made a decision.

'If I can persuade the dealer who employs me that your work is marketable, would you agree to an exhibition at the gallery?' She did not need an answer to her question. She went on: 'Before I speak to my boss I think I should know more about you. Can we meet one evening soon?' She felt disingenuous; her research had informed her about almost everything there was to know about John.

'Of course! I should love to.' They arranged to meet at a bar near the gallery on the following Friday evening which was in two days' time.

There were a number of things about John, which Martina had discovered, which appealed to her. He had been to a well-known public school, progressed to art school in London on a scholarship, was well off because his family was wealthy and had been able to make a career through his talent without having to earn a living. His talent was not in doubt. She also knew he was single, and intuitively, that he found her attractive. He had maintained the professional boundaries which Martina had erected around their two encounters, and for this reason she felt that she might be able to trust him. Unusually for her, she also knew that she found him physically attractive. This was important if there was a possibility that she was going to allow him to invade her carefully constructed solitariness.

In contrast Martina was a stranger to John when they met two days later. He saw her as a business woman who might be able to market his work, but her understated prettiness, which John had had the unique opportunity to scrutinise, while Martina had obligingly sat for him with her eyes closed, had made a profound impression.

The Friday evening gregariousness of the West End bar where they had agreed to meet was gathering pace. They found a table, away from the crescendo of people embarking on weekend socialising, where a waiter brought them a bottle of white wine in a shiny cooler. The waiter placed two tall, spotless glasses on the table, uncorked the bottle with great care and poured a centimetre of wine into John's glass for him to taste before pouring for them both. They clinked their glasses and sipped.

'Tell me about you,' said Martina. John told her all the history of himself which she already knew. He filled in the details about inheriting his parents' wealth after they had both been killed in an air accident five years ago. He had neither sisters nor brothers and, like Martina was alone in the world apart from friends, of whom he had a great many, from school days and college. He expressed enormous pride in his work and knew that he had significant talent which he was anxious to continue to develop; he described himself as a disciplinarian. Work absorbed many hours in his studio with models or visiting people who commissioned him, often using photographic techniques in the houses of his clients and later creating the portraits from electronic images. His reputation among wealthy families, often from abroad, who wanted images of themselves to decorate their mansions, was considerable, as was the income, but he fostered a resentful sense that this was not really his vocation and figurative representations, created in the seclusion of his studio, was where he believed his talent flourished.

Although he was talking about himself and his achievements, he did so in a self-deprecating way. His manner was quiet. He spoke with a faintly patrician accent, carefully shaping his vowels and pronouncing every consonant. He smiled a lot and regularly laughed at his own expense. The effect was beguiling. Martina thought that he was a kind man, possessed of humility. His emerging qualities were intoxicating. He was a real business prospect but as the evening progressed Martina found his company increasingly attractive.

John wanted to know about Martina. She was enjoying John's company and readily told him her life story. She described how much she enjoyed being alone, defensively adding that boyfriends posed a problem for her because she had to sacrifice her solitary idyll to please someone else. She felt selfish as she explained her idiosyncratic habits. John listened intently looking steadily in her eyes; he could not decide if they were blue or grey. Martina paused in her self-justifying narrative.

John took the opportunity to interject. 'I don't usually confess my odd habits so readily, but if I'm not able to spend most of my time alone I get anxious. I think it's a sort of agoraphobia. I've yet to meet anyone in whose company I can stop feeling that I would rather be alone.' He smiled. Martina giggled. 'I think we'll get on well,' she said. They ordered another bottle from the careful waiter.

Had they not taken themselves so seriously they would have slept together, such was the unspoken chemistry between them. Despite the wine Martina was aware that she must do something about getting John exhibited. Her professional self took control. She went home alone and telephoned her boss first thing on the following Monday. To her surprise he agreed to show John's work on Martina's advice alone. Martina was to organise it. It was to be her first opportunity to promote the gallery, upon which much would depend.

The long process of selecting the pictures for the exhibition had to take place at John's studio. Martina and John spent many hours going through dozens of drawings and paintings stored in a loft at the studio. Predictably they became increasingly familiar with each other. But Martina was not ready to sacrifice her carefully constructed singleness and the contentment it created. John, being a considerate man, respected Martina's reserve and did not attempt to intrude. He wanted Martina's portrait to be part of the exhibition and he had an idea for a vignette which involved a series of nine portraits of Martina. She agreed to sit for him but until the project was finished would not say if she would include it in the exhibition.

John's plan was to create seven more profiles of Martina, so he would have four from her right side and four from the left, all with her eyes gently closed and all with her head poised at slightly different angles. He used pencil leads of different hardness and charcoal for two of the portraits. For the ninth picture he sat Martina in a wooden armchair with her arms folded across her chest, her head leaning against the back of the chair, looking into the distance. This portrait was larger than the profiles and designed as a centre-piece around which the eight profiles would be hung. The effect of the finished project was striking, partly because of the clean simplicity of the draughtsmanship, but also the stillness of his subject and the infinitely relaxed poise of the central, seated portrait. As an example of John's most recent work Martina's portraits had to be included in the exhibition. With ten other oil colour and pencil portraits the exhibition was complete. A glossy catalogue was produced and Martina's boss started the complex process of deciding on the possible market values of the individual pictures. Martina's portraits posed a particular problem as they were to be offered as a single work.

Several weeks had passed since the start of the exhibition planning. The gallery was closed to allow a day for the sensitive ritual of hanging John's pictures. This was a process which Martina had come to enjoy, having assisted her employer and various experts, who were usually recruited for the purpose, in the design of how to present previous exhibitions. The prospect of being the subject of the most striking piece in the exhibition had caused Martina some anxiety. Her image had become commodified, a transformation about which Martina had a growing sense of unease. The idea that images of herself should be a source of pleasure to a stranger was discomfiting. Her pleasure in being alone and undisturbed felt threatened, particularly if whoever acquired her was to part with the substantial sum which her employer considered her worth.

The exhibition was hung. The simplicity of the paintings was perfectly in tune with the clean, open space of the gallery with its pure, white walls and shiny, wooden floor. It was too late to ask if her portraits could be withheld from sale. John was too ecstatically pleased with the effect of the exhibition and Martina's employer was too preoccupied with the commercial necessities of launching the exhibition. She kept her reservations to herself but her anxiety did not abate.

Eventually she confided in John. There was to be a preview of the exhibition the evening before it officially opened. A select group of dealers and friends had been invited to be plied with sparkling white wine, dispensed by Martina, as they perused the pictures. During a lull in the hospitality arrangements she found John and explained her reservation about her portraits coming into the possession of a stranger. John was in a state of excitement about the flurry of interest from the dealers. He was taken aback by Martina's anxiety. He had no idea that being the subject of his art could be anything other than flattering, even desirable. His cultivated, considerate self and his affection for Martina made him realise that he must do something to assuage her concern. He considered what this meant. He knew that possessing Martina was something he increasingly wished to do. Perhaps retaining possession of the images he had made of her was critical to the future and if he was not able to absorb her personally into his life, the images of her might be important to keep his intentions alive. As long as he was able to secure a few sales of the other pictures to justify Martina's efforts on behalf of her employer, everyone would be content. He would keep the nine portraits, and in due course, maybe Martina as well.

Martina filled their glasses from the bottle which she held. She smiled and kissed him discreetly on the cheek.

'Thank you,' she said, 'I like the idea of you having me on your studio wall. It will give me an excuse to come and check that I'm properly hung.' John's ready smile broadened. 'You know you'd be welcome. If I promise to go on possessing the portraits maybe you would let me possess you a little, as well.' 'Maybe,' Martina smiled and turned to the gallery to dispense more wine.

So the portraits became the means to the end of allowing some of their self-imposed solitariness to be intruded on by each other. Neither were passionate lovers but neither were they averse to spending time together unclothed, usually at the studio on weekend afternoons. Martina did not relinquish her determination to spend most of her time alone and John could not work effectively unless he was unobserved. The convenient reciprocity of their arm's length relationship suited their idiosyncratic natures. Martina was content with a part-time lover and John felt he possessed enough of Martina to lend meaning to their relationship.

The exhibition at the gallery had elevated John's reputation to that of a sought after figurative artist and he needed to enlarge his portfolio in preparation for future exhibitions. He spent more time with the models in his studio doing what he liked best. He started to turn down the most extravagant of the portrait commissions, which were also the most demanding and troublesome.

Martina's belief in her state of unalloyed happiness with her life continued calmly. She shared her time between her gallery duties, studying emerging contemporary artists, her own contented company, occasional evenings with girlfriends and weekend afternoons in the studio, having sex with John. In the early evening she would seek an expensive restaurant for him to take her to before returning home alone to her solitary, fragrant bed.

John became a famous figurative artist. His most prized possession was his talent; his other possession remained Martina, whom he came to love, but never entirely owned.

Him and Her

They stood on the edge of the forest wrapped in each other's arms, looking across the spring-time valley, bathed in sunshine, lush and coloured a hundred shades of green. They were in love and both knew that they wanted to be entwined with each other for the rest of their lives. It had been a long, sad journey to arrive at this contentment.

Towards the end of the previous summer he had set off, feeling very alone, into the forest, on the edge of which they were standing, and eventually had had to acknowledge that he was lost. The gathering dusk obscured the once familiar landmarks. The woodland was dense and soundless apart from the wind high in the trees. His initial sense of anxiety nagged, making him irritable, insidiously magnifying into a feeling of near panic. He leaned against the rough bark of a huge pine tree, smelling the resin beneath the rough surface. The texture of the bark was alternately jagged and smooth as he ran his hand over the patchwork pattern of the trunk. He craned his neck to see if daylight was visible through the high canopy. Despite the darkness which hid the forest floor, he was able to make out a patch of pale blue through the lattice-work of branches and leaves. The perception of blue was curiously calming; he felt reassured. The damp, semi-putrid smell of the forest floor and the sweet tang of resin enclosed him in a woodland embrace. Sooner or later something would reveal itself; a familiar path or clearing in the forest, would allow him to regain his sense of direction. The denser areas of forest were penetrated by broad, grassy rides, swallowed by the trees in the distance. The paths crossed at irregular angles, which had a gradually disorientating effect.

He walked on at peace with the darkening woodland, his eyesight gradually adapting to the fading light. The distant susurration of the wind, high in the trees, was the only interruption to the quiet calmness which filled the forest. The fading light distorted tree stumps and low growing shrubs, an effect which gave credence to the presence of dryads and mythical things dwelling deep in the deserted woodland. It was the only place for miles around large enough and wild enough in which to get lost. He knew that if he continued to walk for long enough, in any single direction, he would arrive at a road sooner or later, but for now he was content with being disoriented and allowing the forest to swallow him. The fading late summer day had warmed the air; if I am really lost, he thought, a night in the forest held no threat. He secretly welcomed the idea. The reason he had come to the forest in the first place was a kind of escape.

The loss of equilibrium he had felt after the end of a brief relationship was more disconcerting than anything he had felt before. The promise of the slowly warming affection he had felt for a woman, whom he had met by chance in a queue at a supermarket till, was enticing and exciting. His natural caution allowed him to keep a comfortable distance, careful not to hurry their gradual affinity for each other. The summer had been long and warm, a perfect backdrop to their emerging mutual affection. A few weeks ago they had sat in his garden over a long lunch becoming subtly disinhibited by the wine. She had moved from her chair to sit on the bench beside him. She had lent against him, closed her eyes against the late afternoon sun, placed a hand on his cheek and guided his face towards her own until their lips had connected and they kissed, delectably. He wound an arm around her to reciprocate her physical closeness.

'What about doing this with no clothes on?' he asked tentatively.

'I'd like that,' she responded.

They had gone inside, leaving the remains of the meal on the garden table. In the bedroom he had hauled the duvet off the bed; they shed their clothes hurriedly and spent the late afternoon on the cool, cotton sheet, indulging intently in the sensuality of their skin. It was a spontaneous, naked game which worked; they were relaxed, warm and excited by their intimacy, eroticised by day light.

Later she had left without arranging to meet again. He refrained from pursuing her and waited. A few weeks later he received a text: 'Let's do it again'. And so they did. He had taken her out to lunch at a small restaurant where they ate salads and shared three puddings between them with the inevitable bottle of wine. Then they had gone back to the uncovered bed and done it all over again. And again it was an ecstatic encounter; comfortable, languid, funny and erotic.

Afterwards she had said how much she liked being with him but this would be the last time.

'Some time ago I nearly got married' she had explained. 'It came to nothing eventually but we kept in touch and now he's reappeared and wants to try again. And I feel I must; but I badly wanted to see you once more before I disappeared completely.'

She had kissed him briefly, stood up and wandered round the bed towards the bathroom. She was not very tall but beautiful with no clothes on; short dark hair awry, slim-waisted, small-breasted and desirable. Her bum was small and pretty. He heard her showering, sluicing the traces of himself from every crevice, outside and inside. She came back to the bedroom, dressed slowly and sat down on the bed.

'I'm sorry' she said, 'I feel awful about doing this. If it doesn't work out can I contact you again?' He smiled, knowing that was what he longed for, but said nothing. She kissed him again and left. He heard the front door close quietly, turned on his side and dozed, breathing in the smell of her which lingered on the sheet, with the recent sense of her persistent, urgent mouth and prehensile fingers exploring him. What might have been had disappeared as unexpectedly as it had started.

Walking alone in the forest had become a regular means of escape from his confusion at the disequilibrium which the end of this brief encounter had created. He knew the forest was large enough to get lost in and began to feel an ironic sense of relief that he finally did not know where he was. It seemed an appropriate metaphor for his emotional confusion. He wondered why he had felt the initial anxiety as his sense of direction failed him.

He arrived at another cross road between the wide grassy avenues. A hundred yards away a small herd of deer stood silhouetted against the sunset, like sentinels. As he approached them they timidly bounced off into the woodland and became shadows among the trees. He watched them establish a safe distance and settle back to grazing whatever they found on the forest floor, unconcerned by his intrusion. Suddenly they were startled and raced off out of sight. His mobile had made its shrill, metallic noise. He looked at the screen and saw he had been texted: 'Where are you?' She was back in touch. 'Lost. Literally and metaphorically,' he texted back. 'Where?' came the immediate reply. 'In a forest.' 'Stop teasing. I need to see you. Text me when you have found out where you are.'

He abandoned his wandering and set off determinedly in a direction which he hoped would bring him to one of the narrow country roads which wound through the forest. Twenty minutes brisk walk brought him to a clearing in the woodland next to a crossroads where a signpost informed him that he was one mile from the village from where he had started. He stopped and retrieved his phone to text a reply. 'Lost and found. One mile from the village by the cross roads in the forest.' 'Stay there,' came the instant reply, 'I am coming.'

Twenty minutes later a small black car appeared in the distance. She stopped and waved at him to get in. They hugged and he kissed her on the lips. Then he looked at her more closely. Her right eye was half closed and surrounded by a pink and grey bruise. He frowned at her questioningly.

'I know.' She acknowledged his expression. 'I wanted to spend time getting to know him again but all he seemed to want was sex. I said no, not until we had spent more time deciding about our future. And then he hit me. So it's over.' She put the car in gear, turned around and drove slowly back the way she had come. He realised she was silently weeping, tears brimming over her eyelids and overflowing down her cheeks. He put a hand behind her head and massaged the top of her neck without speaking. She slowed down and stopped the car on the verge by a gate into a field, reached into the pocket of her jeans for a tissue, held it to her face and sobbed convulsively for a few minutes. She regained her composure and rested her head on the steering wheel.

'I can't stop crying, ever since he did it, the day before yesterday. I've never felt like this before. I've always coped with stuff and it's really taken me by surprise. I feel anxious when I'm alone and I don't think I slept more than an hour or two last night.'

'What will help,' he asked, 'where are we going?'

She sat up and faced him. 'Can we go to your place? I need to have someone around. I don't feel safe.'

'Of course. Did he just hit you, or anything else?'

'He was quite physical. I had to push him off. That was when he hit me. I fell over. I was really shocked. No one has ever hit me before. I got up and ran out of the house. I was petrified.'

'Come and stay. You can have the spare room.'

The day after they met in the forest he persuaded her to go and see her doctor, partly about her eye but also because she would need to be signed off work. She had become incapacitated by feelings of anxiety and continued to weep silently at frequent intervals. During the following days she would not leave the house alone, ate hardly anything, rarely showered and spoke little. She spent the days and nights in brightly coloured all-in-one pyjamas covered in leopard spots, curled up on the sofa looking at the TV or leafing aimlessly through magazines, withdrawn from the world. She made an incongruous sight; her sad self clad in a comic outfit.

The doctor had offered her counselling, but believing that she would pull herself together in a day or two, she had refused, and now she was falling apart. He did not know how to approach her mute anxiety but liked having her to stay and assumed that in due course she would recover and even resume their old affair. In the meantime he had to go to work but became increasingly anxious about leaving her alone day after day. He called or texted several times a day and if there was not an instant reply became restless until she responded.

A month went by. She had lost weight, had no energy and looked ill; she seemed to shrink inside the engulfing onesie, surrounded by her own feral odour as showering had become too much effort. The autumn had advanced into winter before he persuaded her to come and walk with him in the forest where she had found him trying to escape from the memory of her. She had pulled on various layers over the onesie.

The expedition was not a success. She was too weak to walk far and complained of the cold. They went home and she resumed her vigil on the sofa surrounded by the smell of her own body.

In the middle of the night, during the week before Christmas, he was woken by a movement in the bedroom. She was standing by the bed still in the onesie.

'I want to be hugged,' she said in a small voice.

'It's always good to hug,' he replied. She unzipped the pyjamas and they fell to the floor. She stood by the bed, naked, pale and thin, then lifted the edge of the duvet and slid underneath. She wriggled towards him and they embraced, tensely, with the stale, sourness of her unwashed skin seeping around them. The flood of sensual recollection at the smooth perfection of her skin was intoxicating.

'Relax,' he whispered. Gradually she softened in his embrace and sighed deeply. 'You have to start believing that you are going to get better. May be today was a start.' Her breathing became shallow and regular and he realised she had fallen asleep in his arms.

Waking in the morning together, warm, drowsy and still loosely hugging, was blissful. He dragged himself to the kitchen to make coffee, then the bathroom, showered and returned to the bedroom with the coffee. She had rolled onto his side of the bed and nestled contentedly, still half asleep. Reluctantly he dressed, gathered his things and departed for work. She was asleep again when he left.

When he arrived home in the evening he found her still in his bed, the onesie still on the floor where she had shed it. He picked it up and held it to his face. It smelled pungently of her sweat and other female emanations. He knelt beside the bed and kissed her lightly on the lips.

'Do you know what day it is?' he asked.

She thought for a moment. 'No, I don't think I do.'

'What's happening next week?' She looked mystified.

‘Today is Friday. Work is finished until January. It’s Christmas next week.’ She opened her eyes very wide. ‘We need a plan. First I’m going to run you a bath, then I’m going to cook something, then we can watch a mindless DVD and then it will be bedtime again.’

‘I don’t think I want to sleep on my own. It was a much better night last night. I think I smell.’

‘You smell of you.’ He inhaled the atmosphere under the duvet, got to his feet and went to the bathroom and turned the taps on in the bath. He went back to the bedroom, pulled the duvet off her and lifted her up, cradling her in his arms like a child. He carried her to the bathroom, knelt down by the bath and lowered her gently into the steaming water. Then he washed her hair, got her to stand up and soaped her from head to foot. She sank back into the water and soaked, looking happy for the first time.

‘I want to be looked after,’ she said.

‘That’s exactly what I’m going to do. I’ll be back in a while to get you out. I’ll be in the kitchen.’ He went back to the bedroom briefly, scooped up the onesie, stripped off the sheets in the spare room, and took them all with their fascinating odour to the washer in the kitchen.

He came back to the bathroom with a large towel. She stepped out of the bath into his towelling embrace. He started with her hair, working down her small body, not allowing her to do anything for herself. She sat on the lid of the loo and he dried between her toes.

‘What about clothes?’ he asked.

‘I can’t remember what I brought. I’ll use yours.’ She had made her first decision for several weeks. He returned to his cooking while she rummaged about in his wardrobe. She found a voluminous shirt which came almost to her knees, a thick woollen jumper and a pair of trekking socks. She appeared in the kitchen looking small and chic.

‘You look lovely. Do you know just how effortlessly pretty you are?’

‘Right now I want to be invisible.’ She sat down at the kitchen table and he gave her a glass of white wine.

‘Don’t drink it all at once. You’re not used to it anymore. Now here’s the plan. Every day you’re going to shower. You’re going to eat something at breakfast time, lunchtime and in the evening. Every day we’re going to go out somewhere until you feel confident to go out alone. We need to go to your flat to check it is OK.’

‘Is that the plan? You want me to go back to my flat where that bastard will find me and probably kill me.’ She covered her face with her hands. ‘I want to stay here. I’m so confused how a physical assault could have so completely undermined me. I feel anxious, useless, frightened. Sometimes I think it was my fault because I provoked him. I didn’t know it was possible to feel so unhinged’

‘Of course you must stay here. This was just about you at first,’ he hesitated, gazing at the frying pan where slices of field mushroom were slowly browning, ‘but now it’s about me as well. I want you to stay because I love you.’

‘Just now there’s nothing to love but that’s the best thing I’ve heard since I last saw you and walked out.’

‘There’s plenty to love and I hope you’ll let me. But there are other things you need to do. What about your family and next week, Christmas and all that, and work?’

‘My phone has been dead for ages. I don’t think anyone knows where I am but that’s how I want it to be. I don’t speak to my parents much anyway but I suppose I had better make an effort. I can’t face work yet. I doubt if I have a job anymore. Can we spend Christmas here, doing nothing? I don’t like Christmas anyway.’ He came and sat down next to her, taking her hands in his.

‘Doing nothing with you all next week is my idea of bliss,’ he said. She leant forward and kissed him slowly on his lips. He got up and returned to the cooking. He beat a bowl of eggs and turned them into an omelette filled with the mushrooms. He slid the omelette onto a plate and put it on the table.

‘You have to eat some of it and I’ll have the rest.’ She picked obediently at a small portion of the omelette.

Later they watched a vacuous DVD which was just funny enough to make her giggle, something she had not done for weeks. They went to bed early, at ease with their nakedness. They cuddled in the dark warmth of the duvet and once again the feel of her skin was rapturously sensual and arousing.

‘I love being hugged like this,’ she whispered, ‘but I don’t think I can cope with sex yet. I’m sorry. It’s all too tangled up with what happened. Even the thought of it makes me anxious.’

‘My darling, just being wrapped around you with no clothes on is enough. There’s no hurry. More than anything I want to be with you. We have to get you used to relaxing again because right now you’ve gone tense. Don’t even think about sex.’

On the Saturday before Christmas she dialled her parents’ phone number and waited. She recognised the gruff voice of her Dad when he answered irritably.

‘Oh, it’s you, love. I’ve been trying to contact you for days. Where are you?’

‘I’m sorry Dad. I’ve not been quite well and I’m staying with a friend. I’ve been out of touch with everyone. How are you and Mum?’

‘That’s why I needed to get hold of you. It’s bad news. Are you with your friend just now, because I’m going to have to tell you?’

‘Yes. Go on.’ She knew intuitively what he was going to say and felt her anxiety grow in anticipation.

‘Your mother died. In the night, suddenly. Just didn’t wake up. Ten days ago. The funeral is on Monday.’ She sank to the floor, feeling the tears welling up all over again and sobbed silently.

‘Dad, I’ll come over this afternoon,’ she managed to say, and replaced the receiver. He found her by the phone sitting dejectedly on the floor. ‘My mum has died. Can we go and see my Dad this afternoon. He lives about an hour away.’ He pulled her to her feet and they hugged silently for a long time.

They both knew that they would have to get through the next two days somehow before they could resume their solitary communion. She would need to get clothes from her flat, meet all sorts of people she barely knew at the funeral and be comforted as the bereaved are supposed to be. In reality she had not got along with her parents and since her teenage years her contact with them had been irregular, but her Mum’s death and funeral had to be coped with. The combination of her emotional turmoil and the ambivalence of the feelings evoked by her mother’s death made her feel numb. She found it hard to talk to her Dad and almost impossible to chat to the people who came to the funeral and then the small wake afterwards at her parents’ house. Her Dad had been dry-eyed and solicitous wanting to know about her health but she only managed to say that she thought she was getting better, unable to explain what had happened.

They left as soon as they felt able and drove back to his house. When they arrived she retrieved the onesie from the dryer, went to the bedroom, undressed, climbed into the onesie and got under the duvet. She sobbed into the pillow helplessly for a long time, not able to identify what she was feeling; perhaps it was self-pity, which disgusted her. He came and sat with her in silence, with a book, anxious to be close but leaving space for her to weep alone knowing he was there when she needed him. Eventually she exhausted her tears; her breathing slowed and became regular and shallow again. She slept and slept. Late in the evening he undressed and got into the bed next to her waiting for the morning before enfolding her in his embrace.

She woke late but felt composed, even serene, and padded round the house in the onesie with the hood up, looking like something that lived in the forest. Weeping and sleeping seemed to have had a cathartic effect. They discussed Christmas and agreed to ignore it. He would cook small meals at regular intervals and there was enough wine to keep them going until January. She decided she must phone her father and check he was alright and would be looked after over Christmas. By the evening she had a hollow feeling somewhere inside and realised that she felt hungry for the first time since she had been assaulted.

He practised making omelettes with various ingredients he found in the kitchen putting off the eventual necessity to go to the super market. He tried marmite, bananas, red peppers and celery. He made small quantities every few hours and fed them to her, loving the way her appetite had suddenly become voracious. She allowed herself to be persuaded to get dressed in lots of layers. They drove to the forest and walked through the swampy paths among the leafless trees in the winter half-light.

Christmas came and went. Their contentment in the company of each other hastened the passage of time and it was New Year's Eve almost before they noticed. They went to bed late, slightly drunk, after the TV ceased to entertain them. In the middle of the night he woke aware of his own sexual arousal by her presence in the bed. She lay soundly asleep, lying on her side with her back to him. He gently laid an arm across her. She stirred and turned towards him.

Half asleep she whispered, ‘Let’s do it’. And so they did, slowly and ecstatically, to bring in the New Year.

Linda and Clive

The coach smelled of its passengers, slightly damp and sweaty, interspersed with clouds of pungent perfume. Everyone was dressed in brightly coloured clothes for a happy day out. The seats seemed to be overflowing with overweight, middle-aged adults. There was a noisy chatter, which spoke of the vacant minds of the too loudly laughing, conveying something to the people in neighbouring rows of seats. Having nothing in common with this merry crowd I found a seat near the front of the coach by a window and tried to detach myself from the oppressive bonhomie of the party. The next few hours would be troublesome. I was determined not to be drawn into the vulgarity of the atmosphere and would no doubt be conspicuous by my isolation from the prevailing jollity. Gazing out of the window, trying to look preoccupied, I longed to be somewhere else. The coach pulled smoothly out of the car park and headed on its cheerful way northwards. A volume of Chekhov's short stories, which I thought might insulate me from the intrusive crowd, required more concentration than the crescendo of vacuous chatter would allow. Sleep was elusive with the din of voices. We left the north London suburbs behind and the sunlit countryside sped by. It would not be long before we arrived at our destination and the trippers would disgorge themselves. I planned a rapid exit to avoid having to engage with them in some way.

I had taken a day off from my city accountancy work to fetch a car from Solihull. I did not really need it, but it had appealed to me on a website sale. The coach, which I had never used, seemed to go more or less where I needed to be to collect the vehicle.

After an hour the excitement in the voices of the passengers began to diminish and the initial hubbub became a monotonous babble. The bus had to pick up more passengers from a small town on the route northwards. It came to a stop in an anonymous town centre. The doors opened wheezily. Three people embarked, looking warily at the rows of faces inspecting the new arrivals. An elderly couple held on to each other as they went down the aisle; the man seemed breathless from clambering up the coach steps and had to be helped by his partner. He slumped into his seat and started to cough noisily, turning bright red from the effort. The third, a woman of about the same age as myself, thirty-something, caught my eye and asked if the seat next to mine was free. Undeniably it was, but there were other empty seats, which she ignored.

'Sorry,' she said, 'it just looks safer next to you. I cannot abide coach parties.' I could not help smiling at this kindred spirit.

'That much we have in common,' I agreed, 'only an hour to go.'

Her voice was soft, cultivated, unassuming. I looked at her to see what sort of person had the same aversion to coach parties as me. She was dressed in black, the ubiquitous skinny jeans and a smart-looking, silky, short-sleeved top. She carried a small laptop in a case. Her appearance was unusual, not quite pretty; she had a straight nose in the middle of a face which seemed too narrow. Her large brown eyes were too close together. Her dark hair was short, shiny and untidy confined by a wide blue band. Her mouth was small and mobile, smiling readily when she realised she was being scrutinised. The effect was attractive.

'I hate buses,' she announced, 'but they're cheap and quick. It would be better were it not for all these people and their loud behaviour. They must be on a day trip.'

'They cause a unique kind of suffering,' I agreed, 'but this bus is too convenient – and cheap.' Her presence made me feel less alienated from the crowd. Finding something in common with a stranger was instantly pleasing. It created a sense of solidarity. I decided to find out what else we might have in common.

'Where are you headed? I asked.

'Birmingham,' she said, 'job interview. I do office management and my company wants me to fill a vacancy in the Midland office. I'm not sure I want to live in the Midlands but if the deal is right it might be a worthwhile change for a time.'

'I spent some time in the Midlands a few years ago. It's surprising how different the people are a couple of hundred miles north,' I observed, 'more friendly than the south. It's only when you go north that you realise how reticent everyone is in London.'

'I noticed that. I do half marathons, competitively. It's about the only thing I'm any good at – running. I come home in the first three or four usually. Competing in northern cities is much more relaxed than in London. Something to do with their sense of humour, I think. They take themselves less seriously than in the south.' This, I thought, was probably true.

'I'm going to Solihull to collect a car. I bought it on the internet. A bit risky, I guess, but as long as it works I hope to head back later. It's a sporty thing with two seats and a soft top. Have a lift south if the interview is done. I'll pick you up and rescue you from this claustrophobic bus'.

'For a reticent southerner you don't waste time.'

I smiled. 'My name's Clive. I live in North London. Now I'm not a complete stranger, not one of those people your mother told you never to accept lifts from.'

'She did, too. I've just been to see her, so duty done; I can abandon myself to the excitement of meeting strangers in buses. I think it may be worth the risk. Anything is better than a bus; even being kidnapped by a stranger. There's no one to pay the ransom, anyway. I'm Linda. I doubt if I'll be through the interview before five.'

The rest of the journey passed in trivial chat. We tried to anticipate the interview questions, for which Linda seemed ill-prepared. She was amused by her own dismissiveness. If they wanted her they would have to take her as she was. There was a quiet assertiveness behind her casual approach. We talked about what it might be like to live in Birmingham, my general ignorance about cars and ambition to own one with a soft top ever since being given a lift in an Aston Martin, which had belonged to our neighbour when I was about twelve.

We were deposited in a coach station on the edge of Birmingham, rapidly detaching ourselves from the jovial passengers, and agreeing a place to meet in Solihull at half past five.

The new car was shiny, clean and almost new. Everything seemed to work. It had less than ten thousand miles on the clock. The prospect of driving south with my attractive, new acquaintance in this sporty vehicle was alluring. Our chatter, albeit inconsequential, in the bus had established various preferences we had in common. I, too, was a runner but I did not run competitively. We both found we liked doing solitary things, away from crowds. In particular we disliked things like public transport, coach parties, airport lounges and running clubs. The point of running was to be either alone or possibly with a friend; it was a time to reflect, look at the changing seasons and feel better, physically and psychologically.

We had agreed to meet at a petrol station near the place where we had been deposited by the coach. I would need fuel for the journey south. I drove in at exactly half past five and there she was, waiting on the forecourt. She had a neatly-fitting, expensive-looking, short, black leather jacket over the short-sleeved top. I noticed for the first time how lean she was; an athlete's figure. She installed herself in the passenger seat while I filled the tank and paid.

'Smart jacket' I said as I got back into the car.

'A gift from Birmingham. I decided to take the job' she replied, 'so I thought I deserved a present.'

'Suits you. I like women who wear black. It's a sort of understated fashion.'

'Exactly my intention. I don't like being noticed; I try to stay invisible. If people want to find me they have to look for me.' She smiled. Another thing in common, I thought.

The journey south was congenial. It was a warm summer evening so we put the soft top down and let the wind rush past us. More trivial chat shrunk the time; Linda seemed to enjoy the car observing the complexity of the shiny dashboard, the raucous engine and the alarming acceleration. The landscape swept past. Linda pulled off the hair band and allowed her short hair to be blown around by the wind. We parted company in north London and agreed to meet on the following Sunday morning, before the middle classes emerged with their children and unruly dogs, when I would attempt to be pacer for Linda's training run on Hampstead Heath. To my relief this was a success and during the following weeks became a regular assignation. We scampered across the Heath in sunshine and rain, deliberately splashing through puddles and mud, both looking sweaty and dishevelled, revelling in our muddiness. Our running kit was identical; black leggings and tops, which made us look like twins, both dark short-haired, medium height and lean. We were distinguishable only by our trainers; Linda's were pink and mine were grey. One bright morning, Linda pulled up suddenly, clutching the back of her left thigh. To her dismay she had torn a tendon and was immobilised temporarily. To help with her gradual recovery I offered to go on meeting on Sunday mornings, but for the next few weeks we would walk. Running is obsessive; walking is ruminative. Our congenial chat resumed and became a conversation about each other.

Linda spent the week in Birmingham now, returning to her flat in Kentish Town at the weekends. She had succeeded in buying the flat which was ten minutes from my own in Chalk Farm.

The weeks progressed into autumn and our Sunday walking became a regular event. Brilliant golds, reds and yellows replaced the summer green of the trees; we waded through drifts of fallen leaves and the warmth of summer was replaced by an early autumn chill. The subject of our chatter became more introspective, more intimate, inclined to personal preferences in food and places, the Mediterranean being our favourite for both. We liked contemporary novels. Holidays needed to be active, somewhere hot. We allowed our prejudices to surface and shared them empathetically. Linda had had a series of troublesome relationships with men, some bordering on the abusive, and was hesitant about emotional entanglement. For the time being she had given up on boyfriends. I had had a long relationship which threatened to end in marriage. The prospect of settling down together seemed to take the heat out of the love affair. Rather than entering on the familiar, frenetic wedding planning, we had ended up drifting apart. It had been amicable enough but salutary in its paradoxical conclusion.

By now Linda and I were spending a lot of time together, sharing our mutual ambivalence about partners. On the other hand, we had to acknowledge that the numerous things which we had in common had forged an affection, which had grown between us, and seemed to me was going to blossom into something, sooner or later.

Towards the end of November we were standing on top of Parliament Hill on a fine Sunday morning, the beech trees at the foot of the hill, red and golden behind us, gazing at a hazy panorama of London in the distance. Linda turned to me.

‘I love these walks,’ she said. Our lips met and we kissed, wetly, like teenagers. Then we kissed again, more slowly and carefully. Linda did not use make up. Her black hair and dark eyes needed no emphasis. She smelled deliciously of a faint, feminine perfume.

‘I’ve wanted to do that for a while now,’ I said. We embraced gently. ‘How d’you feel about doing it with no clothes on?’

‘Please don’t ask me to sleep with you,’ she replied, resting her head on my shoulder, ‘I really don’t like waking up with someone else in the bed. In fact I don’t like sharing beds with other people. I haven’t done it very often, but on each occasion when I have I couldn’t believe how I agreed to in the first place. People always look awful in the morning, me too I suspect.’

‘It’s not sleeping I had in mind,’ I explained tentatively. ‘I have become very fond of you over the months, whether you like it or not. Behind your careful invisibility I think you’re terribly attractive and I suppose I want more of you.’

‘I’m fine with that, as long as we don’t have to sleep together, at night I mean. Daylight is good for intimacy. It’s much more exciting when you can see what you’re doing. It makes it more erotic. The best time for sex is Sunday afternoon.’ She giggled and smiled at me. Her huge, brown eyes were bright, her pupils dilated, which made them luminous, like headlights. ‘And it’s Sunday all day today.’

We walked on back to the houses and high streets. We found a restaurant where we ate complicated salads, shared an unctuous chocolate thing for pudding and drained a bottle of red wine, like a loving cup.

When we had paid the bill, and were about to get up from the table, Linda hesitated, put an elbow on the table, rested her chin on the palm of her hand in a thoughtful way, and looking steadily at me, her eyes luminous again, asked coyly: 'Your place or mine?'

Vicky, Viridian and Vermillion

When the twin's Mum, who was called Vicky, discovered that she was going to have twins her first thought had been that she wanted them to be identical, and they were; two tiny, perfect, identical girls, born two weeks early, with surprising ease, on the tenth of September, which was also Vicky's birthday.

She examined them minutely to find distinguishing marks or physical differences by which she would be able to tell them apart. For several days she was unable to tell one from the other until gradually their behaviour, particularly the way they latched on to her nipples when they fed, became the thing that set them apart from each other. Despite their prematurity Vicky discovered that she could breast feed them, which she found deeply satisfying, apart from the soreness. She decided to call them Viridian and Vermilion. She would dress them in bright green and scarlet and that would be how they would be recognised for the whole of their young lives. In due course they would acquire the names of Viri and Mili, (Vermi did not sound right).

Vicky lived with her parents in a council flat on an estate in the middle of London. Her parents did not have high expectations of their only child. The academy school had tried to persuade her that she should apply for university. She had stayed at school long enough to do three respectable 'A' levels but that was the limit of her academic aspirations. University and campus life did not appeal to her. Other wilder and more lascivious entertainment were the focus of her life and readily available in the city where she was born.

Living with her parents was not demanding. They had no idea how or when Vicky would gain some independence. She did not want to live away from the security of the household where she had grown up and felt anchored. She was familiar with all the good, and some of the bad, things which went on in and around the estate. Poverty defined the environment. A small Bengali population kept themselves apart, some not able to speak English. A more extrovert Arab population, mainly from North Africa, provided colour and incessant chatter in the high street. There was unemployment, boredom, drugs and dealers and occasional violence. But the population was stable; many people had lived in the same flat for decades and two or three generations of the same families created a cohesive community. Neighbours looked out for each other and kept the estate safe. Badly paid work was easy to find and Vicky managed to pay her way at home. She was a loving daughter when she was not in the grip of the frenetic preparatory activity which partying with friends regularly demanded. She often helped her Mum in the kitchen and devotedly looked after her Dad, whose health was slowly failing as a result of a life time of smoking. He was incapacitated by breathlessness and spent most of his time sitting in his armchair in front of the TV with a cup of tea and sometimes a can of lager.

Vicky was slim, dark-haired, blue-eyed and lively. She was a party girl. She lived to party and go clubbing with friends. In her teens she had acquired a reputation for getting drunk and out of control. Her parents had given up trying to persuade Vicky to take life seriously. The allure of fun followed by sex was like an addiction. She seemed incapable of sacrificing the possibility of instant gratification for anything more decorous. Early on in her hedonistic career she had brought boys home after her nights out. Her mother had decided that her daughter must have the freedom to do what she wanted but made a rule that if friends stayed they must come to breakfast in the morning. The prospect of sharing tea and toast with the mother of the girl with whom they had spent the early hours trying to have sex was a prospect too onerous for the boys, even without a hangover. So Vicky went home with the boys instead and emerged late in the morning looking dishevelled, as if she had spent the night at an orgy, which was not far from the truth. She slipped quietly into her parents flat, cloistered herself in the bathroom and emerged looking trim and glossy despite her aching head and post-coital soreness. In the process she gained a reputation for being an easy lay, which was not strictly true. Even in her out of control state she retained a discerning approach to which of the available boys she would agree to get unclothed with. The boys had to be clean shaven and short haired. She liked them smart. Long term boy friends had no appeal for Vicky. She shared her sexual favours with a small group of men who competed for her attention, a process which fulfilled Vicky's need to needed. Despite her legendary consumption of exotic cocktails Vicky knew that there were boundaries and risks in the life she chose to lead. She never used drugs or smoked and regularly attended the local clinic to be poked about and tested for the things she was likely to have caught. She became known in the clinic, where the staff liked her and encouraged her to keep attending in a modern, non-judgemental way.

Her recollection of the occasion when the twins had been conceived remained permanently out of focus. She knew she had gone home after an evening of chaotic clubbing with a boy younger than herself, whom she fancied, had sex in a dysfunctional way and a few weeks later found she was pregnant. On reflection she knew that sometimes she had been surprised that it had not happened before. The father was not interested and disappeared from Vicky's life. She contemplated an abortion. As the weeks went by the idea of being a single Mum grew on her; it felt like being a victim and gave her a paradoxical sense of power. She was in control of her life and that of her potential children. The pregnancy created a new and novel identity and a direction in life, for the first time.

Vicky's parents stoically accepted what they knew was an inevitability, her mum secretly relishing the thought of grandchildren. They had not exactly given her an ultimatum; they had been clear that she could stay at home for the pregnancy but once the babies arrived she must find her own place. The social services were supportive and the news that Vicky was having twins pushed her up the housing list. Two weeks before the twins arrived she had been allocated a two bedroom flat on the estate. Vicky's Dad stoically took on the redecoration job, despite his wheezing chest, mainly to remove the traces of the previous tenants. By the time Vicky came home from hospital with her new family, a few days after the birth, because the twins had to spend some time in the special care unit because of their prematurity, she had a flat newly painted white, everywhere.

The transformation from having no responsibilities, no aspirations and next to no possessions, apart from party clothes, was a revelation to Vicky. She launched herself into her new role of housekeeping for herself and the babies with all the energy which she previously expended in the pursuit of pleasure. Very soon she realised that being a Mum came naturally to her. All the intimate tasks which she undertook for the twins were easy. She took pride in keeping them spotless, well fed and blossoming. Most of the time it was exhausting and she found she became anxious about small things which were not in the usual routine. She immersed herself in the work of looking after the twins, living on benefits and having to give up her favourite recreation of partying with her mates. She was happy. Her happiness made her relaxed which transferred itself to the twins. They were easy babies, feeding and sleeping when they should and providing their Mum with endless amusement and contentment.

The mild weather of autumn froze into winter. The estate lost what colour it possessed and took on its seasonal bleakness; the plane trees were bear in the open spaces between the high rise blocks, where stray rubbish blew about in the gusting breeze. The scrubby grass turned into mud patches.

Vicky's parents had spent a large part of their savings on a buggy for the twins, like a chariot with aeroplane wheels. She wheeled them around the estate and up and down the high street, clad in their luminous name colours, in and out of the pound shop and the small supermarket, looking for offers on the basic things she needed to sustain the babies and her. As Christmas approached she knew she must find money to contribute to the celebrations which her parents would arrange with all the vulgar, seasonal extravagance which no one could readily afford.

Christmas came and went with its traditional frippery. Vicky joined in but felt a hypocrite. Since having to provide for her small family she had become acutely conscious of the need for thrift. She allowed herself to join in the celebrations but was uncomfortable with the extravagant commodification of the occasion. She had one gin and tonic on Christmas day which made her feel peculiar, having drunk no alcohol since the twins were born. The twins swigged her milk unaware and slept soundly.

Four months into their contented lives the twins had made Vicky's nipples so sore that the health visitor gave up trying to find more remedies which would allow her to continue feeding and decided the twins must be weaned.

Like everything, else Vicky achieved this with a minimum of fuss, ambivalent about stopping the seductive suckling, but relieved that her nipples stopped keeping her awake at night.

Once the lactation had stopped she started to notice her own body more. A year ago she had been a lissom twenty-four year old; she started to wonder if she would ever regain her former allure to the opposite sex. She decided on a plan. She knew that her mum wanted to be more involved with the twins. Vicky had been so preoccupied with her own maternal ambitions that she had hardly allowed her mum near them. Now that the feeding rituals were simplified she decided it was time to let go. Her mum enthusiastically took on the role of doting grandmother and gave Vicky all the time she needed to start getting herself back into shape.

The party girl friends had not abandoned Vicky. Since the twins were born there had been a constant stream of twenty-something year olds cooing and clucking over them. Some were envious; some amazed, and others alarmed at what might befall all or any of them in due course.

Vicky's best mate since school was Amy. She also had a well-developed sense of hedonism and was enthusiastic for Vicky to re-join the party gang. Amy was the same shape as Vicky had been before the pregnancy, but was blonde. She had the same restlessness as her friend, and equally few aspirations, apart from obsessional clubbing and the pursuit of entertainment. Amy kept herself in shape, also obsessionally, by running every day. Neither girl could afford the gym. She knew that their collective vanity would not allow Vicky to start clubbing again until she had lost her pregnant contours. She decided to set Vicky a goal: she needed to get her bum back into her pre-pregnancy, skinny jeans and persuaded her mate to start running with her. For Vicky, who had never taken exercise in her life, this was challenging. She borrowed the necessary Lycra kit from her friend and painfully traipsed behind her lithe friend through the estate, parks and side streets in the miserable wetness of February. The plan worked. Along with a stringent diet, involving no carbohydrate, Vicky's shape gradually regained its former lissom appearance. Amy ritually measured and weighed her once a week. Six weeks into this regime Vicky dug out her abandoned jeans and, by lying on the floor, succeeded in doing up the waist and pulling the zip up. She inspected herself from front and behind in the bathroom mirror and decided that it was time to see what the boys thought. This would be another challenge. She was aware that no one of her age would be likely to take on a single parent, but her self-esteem would benefit from the attention of the opposite sex.

By the middle of March the weather was milder. The daffodils appeared in the parks and green places on the estate. The herald of spring was exhilarating. The running had not only shed Vicky's maternal weight but she found she was no longer breathless when she ran with Amy. The early spring sunshine and the psychological well-being, the sense of renewal, which the exercise seemed to create, was a euphoric combination. Vicky could not remember being more content in her life. All she lacked was money. It occurred to Vicky that may be she could sell sex, go on the game. She knew that there was at least one local woman on the estate who lived on illicit earnings; a little competition might be good for business. In great secrecy she brought the subject up with Amy who was scandalised.

'Don't you dare,' she screeched, 'it's dangerous, illegal and shameful. I'll never speak to you again if you even think about it.' Vicky was surprised at Amy's vociferous response. She knew that Amy still slept with various men but clearly doing it for money was a cause for indignation. Vicky abandoned the idea and tamely accompanied her friend to the supermarket on the High street, where Amy had a part time job, and asked to speak to the manager.

Work on the tills or stacking shelves was available. It paid the minimum wage for irregular hours. Vicky knew that she could only work a few hours a week without losing her benefits. But because the shop opened at seven in the morning and closed at midnight, and the work was to fill in where there were gaps in the regular staffing, it posed a problem for Vicky's Mum, who provided free child care, because whatever hours were available would be very irregular. On the other hand if the benefits continued to pay for the basic living costs, the earnings would probably cover the cost of a club, and all that went with it, once or twice a month. Vicky took the job and went to speak to her Mum, who was disgruntled at the prospect, mainly because she thought Vicky could do better, and she took the view that respectable mothers did not go clubbing.

So Vicky re-joined the party gang. Her body had become the focus of her attention. She regained her pre-pregnancy weight and succeeded in squeezing herself into the tightest of jeans. Her breasts had changed forever. They were larger than before but Vicky quite liked their new proportions and although not as firm and pert they still retained an erotic contour. Her nipples seemed to be permanently erect, visible through the diaphanous bras she preferred. She launched herself on to the party scene. At the first club night she swallowed three cocktails in quick succession and thought she was going to pass out. Amy came to her rescue in the loo and guided her back to the frantic, cacophonous dancing. She went home to her flat alone and sober in the early hours, chastened and feeling guilty, longing to see the twins, who were at her Mum's flat. As she fell asleep she reflected on her life and all the good things which contributed to her happiness; the twins, her Mum, the flat, the job, Amy and her friends. She made a decision. The twins mattered more than anything else. She would give up alcohol. The decision gave her an unfamiliar sense of virtue and she woke a few hours later, feeling even happier than usual, with the sense that she was more in control of more of her life than ever before.

To her dismay the twins were not with her on the morning after her return to partying. She realised she had sacrificed the most exquisite part of the day to her headlong hedonism. The mornings were an important part of the ritual of motherhood. Once awake she had to have the first cup of tea and then went to the bathroom and ran a bath. She always anticipated the wakening stirrings of the twins in their cots. She would lift them, hug them, kiss them and divest them of their night clothes and nappies. She would take them to the bathroom where all three would wallow in the bath rejoicing in their shared nakedness. From the outset of this ritual Vicky was astonished by the sensuality of the babies. As the months went by they became old enough to sit and support themselves in the water between her thighs, encircled by her legs, and then clamber on her tummy and grasp at her breasts. She relished the sensual, naked contact which was intensely pleasurable and often erotic. Being unsure if the particular sort of pleasure she derived from being in contact with her babies perfect skins was quite right she rationalised it by reminding herself that this blissful hour of the morning would soon pass into the twin's history, and the daily encounter was a transient source of delight and love for all three of them. She tried to make time slow down and protract the months of dependent baby life. None of them would ever experience this particular physical and psychological playtime euphoria again. Bath time was the priority and nothing would deprive Vicky of the indulgence again until the twins were too old to share their bath with her. She knew that she had to maximise her baby-time before it was over so she allowed herself one hour a day to scamper around the streets, usually with Amy, while her Mum had the twins; she made her excuses to the manager at the supermarket and she suppressed the clubbing instinct for the time being.

Vicky's life adopted a timetable – waking, bathing, dressing and feeding. Installed in the chariot she wheeled the babies to her parents' flat to hear the gossip and make sure they were still alive, and then to the High street for her frugal shopping. They returned to the flat for lunchtime and more feeding, naps and domestic chores, because Vicky aspired not just to be a model Mum but was fiercely house proud. The flat was pristine. As the weather warmed in early summer the inner city denizens ritually re-clothed themselves in scanty spring time cotton, and Vicky was no exception. Now that she could fit into her skinny jeans and a tee-shirt she flaunted her newly reclaimed shape, secretly enjoying the attention she attracted from the men loitering outside the betting shop in the High street, who turned to look at her bum as she wheeled the buggy past them along the pavements and park paths. Thoughts of men competed ineffectually with her overwhelming devotion to the twins. She fantasised about an idealised mate who would become a parent to her children and at the same time be a gentle lover. She reminded herself of the many things which contributed to her happiness and decided that men were probably not among them; she knew that this particular paragon was elusive but that did not stop her from wondering where she could look for one.

The twins grew at an alarming rate as did their small personalities. Every small accomplishment and idiosyncrasy filled Vicky with disproportionate excitement. The twins were smothered in kisses and love with every small novelty. The warmth of summer succeeded spring. Vicky's routines were uninterruptedly busy and as August arrived she realised with amazement that in September they would all three celebrate their first birthday together. Vicky's mum had anticipated this event and started to bake; she was expert at cakes. The girlfriends were invited and arrived bearing bottles of fizz. Three birthday cakes, over flowing with unctuous fillings, graced Vicky's table. The twins were covered in cake, and Vicky was slightly the worse for fizz, when she was suddenly struck with a new ambition inspired by the cakes. Before her partying days, before she was twelve years old, she used to spend every Sunday morning at home with her Mum learning how to make and bake cakes. She had not forgotten how to do it. She knew the local council ran courses where she could gain some more sophisticated skills and then she would start a business, baking for other people. The project pleased her immensely. She would not have to sacrifice an hour away from the twins, apart from attending the course, and she would create a business from the kitchen of her flat.

By the time the twins were two Vicky had mastered all sorts of different sponge mixtures, a huge variety of fillings and icing techniques, wedding cakes, birthday cakes and of course cup-cakes and biscuits, for which she knew that she would find a ready market. The course prudently included advice on how to price the resultant confectionary and the requirements of health and safety, should the trainee bakers want to start a business.

Publicity on the estate was easy. Word of mouth created a market and every week Vicky had new orders. Her starting prices rapidly inflated as her project expanded. She recruited her Mum to help and keep an eye on the twins who were mobile and full of curiosity, not all of it innocent. She sold the cakes for cash and thought it unnecessary to inform the tax man, at least for the time being. Another layer of happiness seemed to have settled on Vicky and her charmed life. She felt successful and excited. The creativity which went into her cake making felt deeply satisfying.

In due course the twins had to start school. They had been to play groups from an early age but were always accompanied by Vicky. For the first time in their short lives she would have to relinquish her family to the care of a stranger. The prospect of separation caused Vicky an unanticipated anxiety. The twins had grown into identical, diminutive versions of herself. They had straight dark hair and blue eyes. They were thin girls with their mother's restlessness and energy. They were articulate infants because Vicky had nattered to them ceaselessly for the whole of their lives. On the first day at the school, which was in the middle of the estate, Vicky presented them at the school gates to their new teacher, dressed in their habitual green and scarlet jeans and tee shirts, the significance of which she explained to the bemused teacher. They disappeared inside the school building. Vicky turned away and felt suddenly miserable. She hurried back to the flat and had to blot the tears which spontaneously appeared. She had no idea that separation could be so painful. Remorsefully she consoled herself with the probability that the girls would not miss her at all. She distracted herself with the preparation of the next batch of cup-cakes, counting the minutes before she could go and fetch the twins from the school, becoming increasingly desperate to know how they had spent the morning.

Vicky stood impatiently at the school gates. Punctually the kids came bursting out. The twins bounded up to Vicky brandishing the cardboard and paper creations which they had made during the morning.

'Mine's a rabbit,' announced Viri. 'And mines a duck' added Mili. They thrust their animals at Vicky and took no more notice of them. Vicky bent forward and hugged her girls.

'You're very clever, both of you,' said Vicky. 'Tell me what you did'.

'We had orange juice,' Viri advised. And that was the sum of the information which Vicky had to console herself after the morning of agonising separation.

The twins loved their new school and enthusiastically engaged with the projects and preparations which their teacher dreamed up week by week. Like true twins they did everything together; sat together, played together, ate together and were as inseparable as best friends, which is what they were. While the twins were entertained at school Vicky applied herself to the making of cakes undistracted by her children. The business grew and Vicky knew she would have to decide whether the project needed to move onto a grander scale or be kept within the confines of her council flat kitchen. She decided to consult her friend, Amy.

Amy was still a party girl, averse to responsibility. She loved Vicky and the twins and was a regular, uninvited visitor to the flat. She liked to be consulted about Vicky's plans and anxieties and had formed clear views about the direction of Vicky's life.

'If you turn it into a proper outfit I 'fink you'll spoil the fun. You'll 'ave 'elf and safety round before you can say knife; then there's the tax man. You got the twins to look after, 'an all.' Vicky knew ambition came at a price. She bowed to the wisdom of Amy.

'Wot you really need is a bloke!' Vicky knew this was true. More than anything she missed the sensual contact of skin. The twins were too big to get in the bath with her now and the bath time rituals had become a thing of the past, and anyway they had their own bath-time entertainment. If she woke in the night she longed to be hugged but her nights remained stubbornly solitary. She had looked at dating web-sites but they were full of randy looking men who she persuaded herself would not be interested in a single Mum. From time to time Vicky would eye up the Dads waiting at the school gates. They were an unpromising bunch, most of whom she knew, married and mostly unemployed. Although surrounded by friends and parents, all ready to help and look after her, the man she needed remained elusive. Vicky enjoyed life too much to allow the absence of a man to intrude on her happiness but she knew that the longing for intimacy would not go away.

‘We need a plan’ Amy announced. ‘You’re thirty in September, I been countin’. We gotta find you a bloke before then’. She looked pensive. ‘We need to cast the net a bit wider. We need a bloke wot likes cake and kids.’ Being of her generation Amy was a social media expert, which was her only technical accomplishment. She decided to put out messages to trawl for a single, cake loving man, hoping that she would not be misinterpreted. To Vicky’s relief Amy received plenty of saucy responses but no one interested in rescuing her from her manless state. She also knew secretly that the harder she looked the less likely it was that she would find what she was looking for; everything in her life had happened by chance or opportunism. If a man was going to materialise it would have to happen by some timely coincidence.

The birthday came and went and no man had presented himself. The twins were due to start their second year at the school after the summer holiday. They had a new teacher and their school day had become less playful and more purposeful. The twins took this in their stride. They had gained all sorts of independence and needed Vicky less and less to help with getting ready. Dressing in the morning was simplified by their habitual colour code. Vicky just made sure they did not forget to wash while they splashed in the bath and tidied their straight, dark hair, sometimes tying it back if the girls preferred. The walk to school took five minutes and Vicky, now used to not having the girls around would hurry home, take herself out for her habitual run, collecting Amy on the way if she was not at work, and get back to her kitchen where the cake orders showed no sign of abating.

One morning in the middle of the school term, when Vicky was up to her elbows in cake mixture, her mobile started its tinkling noise which meant she had a call not a text. She hurriedly wiped her hands and peering at the screen saw to her surprise that the school was calling. She immediately thought something awful must have happened. The school had never called. The head teacher introduced himself, apologised for calling and explained that the twins were behaving oddly, refusing to do anything which they were asked and not answering when they were addressed; most out of character, he concluded. Vicky abandoned the kitchen and ran to the school. The head teacher, a middle-aged, balding man with a kind face, had taken the twins to his office where they sat side by side looking angelic, but quite mute. The new class teacher joined them. Vicky looked at her girls and started to giggle. The effect was infectious and in no time the girls were convulsed in squealing laughter.

Vicky recovered her composure and smiled at the class teacher, who smiled back. He was sandy-haired; brown eyed, wore rimless spectacles and was about the same age as Vicky. He seemed readily amused at the twin's hysterics.

'They're wearing each other's clothes and they won't answer to each other's names,' explained Vicky. The twins went into renewed peals of laughter. The head teacher looked mildly embarrassed and suggested that they returned to the class room. Vicky introduced herself to the class teacher and started to apologise.

The class teacher, who introduced himself as Paul, was greatly amused by the event. 'I suppose I should be impressed by how completely they carried it off,' he said, 'but it was so out of character I got alarmed at first. Normally they're so good. You have two clever, pretty daughters, Vicky. I'm sure we shall manage now they've been found out. Clearly I need to get to know them better.' He looked at her steadily and smiled. The effect was attractive and Vicky smiled back, unhesitatingly. She had the fleeting impression that she was being flirted with.

Later on when Vicky collected the girls from the school gates Paul came out as well.

‘So it’s all back to normal but I’m still not sure how to tell them apart other than by the colour of their clothes,’ he said, ‘can you give me a clue?’ Vicky thought for a moment, looking fondly at her girls who watched the grown-ups steadily. ‘Not really,’ she replied, ‘it’s easier when they’re in the bath because they each have a mole, in different places. Otherwise there isn’t much difference but Mili is quieter than Viri, usually. Anyway, I’ll check on the dress code in future.’ She smiled at Paul, who smiled back and once again Vicky felt a slight, flirtatious frisson.

Vicky marched the twins home pretending to be angry, but it did not work. They giggled all the way home. As usual there were cakes for tea. The twins sat at the kitchen table munching. Viri looked at Vicky.

‘Our teacher’s nice,’ she said, ‘D’you like him, Mummy?’

‘Yes,’ she said, ‘he seems really nice.’

‘I think he likes you,’ added Mili, and went into another fit of giggles with Viri. Vicky was taken aback. She could not believe her girls were so perceptive

The encounter at the school gates made Vicky wonder if what she had felt was real. She was mildly perturbed that whatever had happened had not gone unnoticed by her daughters. It made her reflect. She had grown up on the estate; thought of herself as working class. Her youth could not be described as deprived but she was certain that she and her parents were poor. Life had always been hand to mouth with nothing left over and now she was dependent on benefits. It had never occurred to her that may be men from the middle classes, professional people, might find her attractive; she was sure that she was too ordinary. Undeniably Paul was a nice looking man but she was not sure if teachers were supposed to have affairs with the parents of the children who they taught. She would have to consult Amy.

Amy was unequivocal. 'Go for it, love. 'Course they can 'ave affairs wiv' anyone they like. They ain't doctors or nuffink.'

Vicky contrived to spend time at the school. She was not inclined to join committees and did not want any additional responsibilities. She needed a way to be around her quarry, Paul. Months went by without plausible excuses to be at the school and Vicky began to give up the plan. The cake making kept her busy and she started to explore new types of cake to expand her repertoire. In her researches she came upon Simnel cake, with its association with Easter. The school was going to put on a concert at the end of the spring term for which the girls had been learning Easter songs, some rather religious but also songs about chocolate and chickens. A week before the end of term, and the concert, Vicky asked to see Paul after school. She chatted about the girls and their new songs and eventually got round to explaining that she baked cakes for people. Would the class like a Simnel cake for the concert day? Paul was clearly pleased to see Vicky and brought her into the class room to show her the Easter preparations and some of the work the twins had been doing.

'Are you a full time Mum' he asked, 'or do you have to do a job as well?' This was Vicky's chance.

'I spend a lot of time baking cakes for people's parties and stuff. It's like a small business but I only do it for a bit of cash. The rest of the time I spend with the girls. Family time is really important because they don't have a Dad. I spend every day at home cooking and being there for them. So if you need a cake you know where to come.' She smiled at Paul in what she hoped was a welcoming sort of way.

'My birthday is in the Easter holiday. I'll need a cake for that. But the Simnel cake idea is brilliant. You'll be at the concert I guess. Will you be able to bring it with you? And then I'll place the birthday cake order. I really appreciate the thought. See you next week; I'm looking forward to it already.' So am I, thought Vicky. The bait was cast. She would get him round to the flat to show him the birthday cake designs.

After the Easter songs had been sung to the parents Paul gathered his class for the Simnel cake treat. He made everyone sit down and explained at length about Simnel cake and Lent and Easter and how Vicky had made a special twenty-first century version of an historic cake for the class. Vicky had brought paper plates and ceremoniously cut and distributed the cake to the over-excited kids who devoured it completely. It was extremely sweet and probably quite unsuitable but as there was not a trace of it left neither Paul nor Vicky much minded. The class went home early to start the holiday and Vicky stayed on with the twins to help clear up.

'That was a great success,' announced Paul. 'I think it would be good to do it again if we can think of an excuse.'

'The next excuse is the birthday cake. You could come and see the designs at the flat and then I'll show you how to make it,' suggested Vicky. Paul looked at her, only half smiling.

'Is that a promise? A cake making lesson?' He sounded enthusiastic. 'I've never made a cake.' Vicky saw her chance.

'Who's coming to the birthday party?'

'Actually no one yet, apart from my mum, who will probably want to come round. But there's no one at home. I live on my own.'

'Come on Sunday. I'll do a bit of lunch and we can spend all day making cakes.' Vicky held her breath. Paul smiled, looking at her very directly as if trying to fathom something.

'I'd really like that' he said, realising the tension was building. 'See you on Sunday,' he added casually.

As they walked back to the flat Mili said very seriously, 'Is our teacher coming to stay in the holidays?'

'I don't think he'll be staying,' said Vicky, 'but he's coming to see us on Sunday,' she added, feeling triumphant.

Paul arrived in the middle of the morning on Sunday. He hugged Vicky briefly and kissed her on both cheeks in a chaste, middle class way. Vicky was unaccustomed to this style of greeting but had no objection. She equipped him with an apron and set about showing him the basics of cake making. Then she got the recipe books out and told him to choose a design. He picked an unctuous chocolate confection which Vicky had not made before and she set about instructing Paul in a systematic way.

They chatted about each other. Vicky told him about herself and her parents. She omitted the finer detail of her wild days before the twins arrived or anything about how she had become pregnant. Paul lived in Streatham in a flat he had been able to afford to buy. When he was not at school his main preoccupation was music. He played the violin with an amateur orchestra. Lunch was full of hilarity with the twins who thought it was wonderful that their teacher should be sitting at their kitchen table. Eventually they disappeared to their bedroom to play. The flat was full of the smell of baking cake and chocolate, Paul said: 'Vicky, this has been a lovely way to spend Sunday but I think it's more than about making cakes.'

'Yes,' said Vicky, 'I was sort of hoping it might be.'

'The problem is,' Paul went on tentatively, 'I can't really be seen to be socialising with the parents of the kids I teach. Someone's bound to cause trouble. But I can't pretend I wouldn't like to see you again.'

'Well,' said Vicky, 'that makes two of us.' Paul arranged his elbows on the table and rested his chin in his hands. He looked steadily at Vicky who returned his gaze, smiling a little. 'So what's the answer?' she asked. Paul looked pensive.

'During the holidays there are matinee concerts at the Festival Hall. Do you think the twins would like a few outings? For now we need to be innocent and discreet.' Needless to say neither Vicky nor the girls had ever been to a concert and the whole idea sounded unlikely to Vicky, but if it was a way to see more of her alluring new friend she really did not mind. The cake was done and Vicky busied herself extracting it from the tin and placing it on a cake stand. In due course it was time for Paul to leave. The twins demanded to know when he was coming again. 'We shall see Paul soon. We are going somewhere special with him,' promised Vicky, knowing that it would have to happen now. Paul said goodbye to the girls and then turned to Vicky and hugged her a little longer than he needed to, then he kissed her again on each cheek.

'I'll call you tomorrow with a plan.'

'And you'll need to collect the cake when I've finished it off.'

Paul disappeared down the stairs leaving Vicky feeling languid and full of a pleasurable sort of longing. She wanted the twins near her because she needed to share her happiness.

'Come here girls. I need you to help me clear up. We need to ice the cake and make a chocolate filling for it. Did you like having your teacher to lunch, he's fun isn't he? He's going to take us out next week.' They chattered away and soon it was time to turn the TV on because that was what Vicky permitted her girls on Sunday evenings. The girls had supper and then Vicky put them to bed, as lovingly as ever, with a long story. She was too excited to watch TV so she phoned Amy and breathlessly told her all about Paul. Amy was an impetuous girl and did not want her best mate to waste time.

‘I told you, you lucky slag,’ shouted Amy who was in the pub, ‘Make sure you let me know when you want the girls lookin’ after. You gotta’ shag him soon; I’ll ‘ave the girls over. Let ‘im know you’re for real; you still gotta’ life, darlin’. That’s the best news since Christmas’.

Paul booked the matinee. On a Thursday afternoon Vicky walked the twins across Westminster Bridge and down the Embankment. They found Paul in the foyer. He took them to the bar and they had drinks before entering the auditorium. Neither Vicky nor the girls had been to the Festival Hall before and for Viri and Mili it was an overwhelming experience. The scale of the space in front of the stage was enthralling and they sat in well behaved silence between Paul and Vicky, amazed by everything they saw.

‘Now girls,’ said Paul, as the orchestra started to assemble on the stage, ‘I’ll tell you what’s going on. That platform at the front of the stage is for the conductor. He comes on last and then waves his arms about to start the concert and help the musicians get the music right. On his left are the violinists and on the right there will be violas which are similar to violins. At the back are the wind instruments, that’s oboes and clarinets and flutes. In the middle is the tympani. That’s drums mainly. On the right and at the back are cellos and double basses, like huge violins, and the brass. That’s trumpets, trombones and French horns. Now, here’s the conductor. He always gets applause and then he’ll start.’ The orchestra played short, easy to listen to pieces, as the concert was designed for children. They did Ravel, Debussy and then Sati with curious, haunting melodies. During the interval they had ice-creams and watched the barges on the Thames slowly heading up the river. Soon the concert was over and they drifted out to the Embankment and wandered about among the crowds and mime artists. The twins were excited and rushed about, craning over the railings at the River. Viri asked excitedly, 'Can we come again tomorrow?'

'No, love, you can't have treats every day,' said Vicky.

'No,' added Paul, 'but if your Mum says yes, we can come again next week.'

'Can't wait,' concluded Viri and rushed after Mili into the crowd.

'What do you think?' asked Paul, 'shall we do it again?'

'Love to,' said Vicky. The following week they did it again. After the concert, while the girls ran about in the sunshine on the Embankment, Paul and Vicky sat on a bench and watched the River. Paul turned to Vicky, looking earnest.

'Vicky, I really want to go on seeing you. I love the twins and I really like being with you, but it will be a bit complicated. Term starts again next week but I'm leaving the school at the end the summer term. I got offered a job in an Academy school south of the river. Once I stop looking after the twins it'll be simpler. But what about you?'

Vicky smiled and thought about her phone call with Amy.

'You're the first bloke I've seen since the twins were born. I'll still be here at the end of term if you're still interested. The girls will talk about you anyway. So maybe it's better to have a break. I don't think there'll be many blokes queuing up at the door of a single Mum. You may be taking on more than you bargained for, but it's up to you.' Paul leant forward and kissed her briefly on her lips.

'Let's stay in touch. Once I've left the school I'm going to come after you. Promise you'll still want to see me.' Vicky smiled again and thought how much she would like to follow Amy's advice.

'Promise,' she said, and returned the kiss.

Simon and Sue

The counsellors were like removal men, always wanting people to move on. Simon had been persuaded to see the counsellor because he was bereaved and felt emotionally incapacitated, finding himself tearful in all sorts of inconvenient situations. His grief was an invisible appendage which went everywhere with him. If he moved on, as the counsellors advised, his appendage would come with him. The appendage, although not visible, was made of sadness and wired to his waking thoughts. It was often provoked by unpredictable encounters and events and made itself felt in Simon's unspoken behaviour. He would feel a tension in the muscles of his face, which would prevent him from speaking in case he dissolved, change the pattern of his breathing or suddenly make silent tears appear in his eyes.

Simon grieved for a woman, called Sue, with whom he had lived for twenty childless years. She had died suddenly. He had woken in the middle of the night, his arms around her, sensing an unfamiliar coldness. The unspeakable realisation of her lifelessness gradually penetrated his consciousness. It was the worst moment of his life. The coroner attributed Sue's death to a problem with the conduction of the electrical impulse in her heart muscle, which had caused it to stop beating, despite the fact that Sue had never been ill in her life. Simon thought the cause of death recorded on the death certificate was implausible, and so he was left with the ineffable fact of the death of the woman he loved with no demystifying label for the cause.

Sue had been a very beautiful woman. Few people knew this because outwardly she looked ordinary and liked to dress in a way which deliberately did not attract attention. She liked to feel invisible. She had short, straight, dark hair; large brown eyes and a small mouth. She had always been thin, a fact she successfully disguised beneath loose fitting, pastel coloured clothes. From the first occasion when Simon had been in a bed with her he realised that she was ravishing when unclothed. A large part of Simon's love for her had been because of the way she kept her physical perfection a secret. She shared this attribute with him alone. The charm of her company had been alluring; she was guileless and impetuous in the way she used to make instant decisions about everything. She was permanently amused by life's vicissitudes and regarded regret as a waste of time and emotion. She believed in a form of predestination. There was no way to change the direction which life took. Life was for living and she loved doing it with her long term lover, a fact which made Simon love her more. Their childlessness had been a problem when it first became apparent that Sue was not going to conceive easily. They had got as far as consulting a gynaecologist about their options, which was enough to persuade them both that either conception needed to happen spontaneously or not at all. Sex remained a cornerstone of their relationship and they had agreed that if it ever died their relationship would die with it, so they made a conscious effort to remind each other of the need for regular, joyful physical indulgence, but Sue did not become pregnant.

Sue had been cremated. Dozens of people came to the crematorium where a dry-eyed humanist talked about Sue and her life, her work as an assistant at an art gallery and her abiding devotion to Simon. Two of her girlfriends from work had added short, tearful eulogies. Later they had all gathered at a local pub and become drunk in a maudlin way in the middle of the afternoon. A few days later Simon was at home with the earthly remains of his lover in a wicker casket unable to stop weeping. The eulogising girlfriends had called in on a pastoral mission, found Simon in an emotional abyss and persuaded him to see a counsellor.

Moving on, as the counsellors advised Simon to do, seemed illogical and he did not wish to do so, even if he knew how. Closure was another annoying term the counsellors used. Apart from its euphemistic, transatlantic derivation he did not see how this was a realistic object. It implied a conclusion; but Simon had no desire to conclude his life with Sue. He needed to learn how to live with her not being there, to accept her absence, and control his wayward appendage. His contented existence with Sue was as indelible in his memory as the ink which the woman at the registry office had used to sign the death certificates. He had no wish to erase a moment of their lives. But his sadness enclosed him like a second skin and stopped him from feeling anything else. The counsellor wanted him to work harder with him; to help himself. But it felt to Simon like helping the counsellor to move on. So he remained harnessed to his appendage, wrapped in sadness.

Simon's colleagues at work encouraged him to stay away until he felt ready to return. The desired readiness was elusive so Simon decided to see if he had attained the necessary readiness by trying to work. He was a partner in a small law firm which handled mainly domestic issues; conveyancing, the acquisition of freeholds, wills, probate, divorce and disputes between neighbours. He liked his role among his clients and approached the work from the stand point of kindness. His object was always to do the optimum good for his clients and minimise any consequent harm to anyone else. There was great satisfaction to be derived from the appearance of successive generations of the same families requesting his services; he considered the continuity of the care of his clients a virtue in the same way that doctors did. Immersing himself in the problems which other people brought him was a useful distraction from his emotional turmoil. He wondered how true it might be that the experience of his own grief would enable him better to empathise with the grief he encountered among his clients, who brought the wills of their deceased relatives for him to administer. There was clearly a risk that his own psychological state would be an obstacle to responding to his equally grief-bound clients with appropriate words of consolation. But it was a risk he was prepared to take and wondered if there was anything to be learnt from how others handled their loss. Recognising the sadness of other people was easy enough. He thought the problem would be his own affective response which would inevitably be confounded by his feelings of sadness. The counsellors had not succeeded in helping him to diminish the episodes of overwhelming sadness, which regularly afflicted him and made him feel like weeping, usually at the most inappropriate moments. He knew that life must go on and decided to seek a way to accept his grief without the help of the counsellor.

Work became a daytime panacea. Other people's problems were more interesting than his own and displaced his misery. In the evening he cooked, listened to the radio and read voraciously, which was how it had always been. The television had never interested him or Sue. The nights remained a dilemma. He woke at three in the morning and watched the hours on the bedside clock until five when he knew he fell asleep, because he woke again at seven. The absence of his lover in the bed was agonising. Their relationship had always been tactile and the warm sensuality of Sue's skin at night had been a source of amazement to him from the first time they took their clothes off in each other's company. His longing for her physical presence was fathomless and painful. There were some nights when life seemed to have lost whatever purpose it ever had and his perplexed brain invented suicidal thoughts. His rational self told him that this was self-pity, which he despised. He discovered that the BBC world service provided temporary respite from his dark ruminations, in the early hours, with bizarre stories from strange places, reaffirming that life was going on all over the world, his own life included.

Weeks of grief turned to months. The emotional fragility, which regularly intruded, did not seem to lessen. Simon began to wonder what was supposed to happen next. He decided to look up ways to grieve and discovered that the process had been codified but did not seem to correspond with his own experience; five stages of grief had been identified by the experts so he tried to work out where he had got to in this process. He was not aware that he denied the fact of Sue's death, which was supposed to be the starting point; he had never wondered if there was anything which he could have done to prevent it; he was not depressed, just sad. He regularly felt angry, mainly about having to live without his lover, but he was not sure if that is what was meant as a stage of grief. The final stage was acceptance but he seemed to be stuck with the impossibility of accepting the inescapable fact that Sue no longer existed. She remained vivid and sensuous in his head. He was uncertain about what it all meant and indeed if it mattered; it certainly did not help.

On the anniversary of Sue's death Simon was cooking at home in the evening reflecting sadly how wonderful it would be if she was there with him, chatting about her day at the gallery. Something reminded him that her ashes remained in their casket, neglected in the bedroom, where he had left them months ago. He decided he needed the ashes close to him and brought them downstairs to the kitchen where he placed the casket on the surface next to the stove and opened it. Inside the casket was a bag made of some densely woven material containing the ashes. He hauled the bag out, undid the cord which kept the bag closed, and immersed his hands in his lover's ashes. They felt coarse and granular interspersed with a fine powder. He looked down at her and tears ran down his face and dripped into the pale remains of the woman he loved, which made him wonder if his behaviour was morbid but did not really mind. He decided it was time to do something with her. Incarceration in the casket felt wrong. Sue had been too much of a free spirit to be confined in this sentimental receptacle.

Exactly where he should scatter the ashes needed careful consideration. The thought evoked waves of complex emotion. Contemplating the thought of doing the scattering renewed Simon's tearfulness but it felt different. There seemed to be a sense of something like happiness, or relief from something onerous, associated with the prospect. He decided he needed to revisit the places where they used to spend long summer days walking across the fields and hills, from pub to pub, in the Chiltern Hills, near where they had lived. He was certain Sue would have liked the idea.

As spring advanced to summer, and the weather warmed the air, Simon chose a week day to absent himself from the office. He wanted to dispose of his lover when the hills were not cluttered with weekend walkers. It was a Wednesday and the sky was blue from horizon to horizon. It was going to be a hot day. This was important because Sue was averse to the cold in winter so setting her free needed to be somewhere warm. He packed a frugal picnic, with a bottle of wine and the casket, in a rucksack and drove to the hills.

He followed a familiar track which he soon abandoned and headed up a grassy hillside. He came to a fence beyond which was woodland where he installed himself on a tuft of grass. A gentle, westerly breeze made waves in the colourful, summer grass on the hillside beneath him. Simon realised that he was hungry so he started on the picnic and opened the wine bottle. When he had had a glass or two and finished the food he extracted the casket and pulled out the bag with the ashes inside. He stood up to consider the view but realised that his vision was obscured by tears which gathered in his eyes at the thought of what he had come to do. Opening the ash bag, he dipped his hand into the contents and flung handful after handful of his lover's ashes across the hillside. The breeze caught the fine, white powdery ash and bore it skywards. The rest of Sue's remains were lost in the grass. When he had emptied the bag he sat down again with the rest of the wine. He wept for a time in the sunshine with a black sense of despair then lay down in the grass and fell asleep.

When he woke the sun was low in the sky but the air still felt warm. He sat and gazed at the distance realising how much he loved Sue, and always would, and how good that felt; and that thought made him happy.

Deborah

In nineteen sixty-five, when Deborah was fourteen years old, she decided that she enjoyed learning about grammar. She would never admit this to her friends because she knew she would be laughed at. Understanding how sentences were constructed, and the role of different kinds of words, seemed a curiously introspective and intrinsically interesting process to be able to master.

The teacher of grammar at her school in North London was a tall, ascetic man, called Mr Booth, who was devoid of humour. He was a grammarian and a didactic pedant. He imparted to his pupils precisely what he believed that they should know, neither more nor less, in precise, unhesitating language and expected his pupils to comprehend instantly. His lessons were as dry as the Atacama Desert. His appearance matched his approach to the curriculum. He wore a faded tweed suit, which had become leaden with chalk dust, over which he draped a black academic gown. His face was long, bespectacled and expressionless. He reminded Deborah of a picture of a Dodo which hung on her bedroom wall.

Deborah, like nearly half of her class, was Jewish, the daughter of parents who had fled from the Nazis before the war, leaving her grandparents behind who had succumbed in a Nazi death camp. None of the families of these girls were particularly observant in their Jewishness. They had in common a middle class aspiration that their children should excel at something and progress seamlessly to university, where they would obtain a degree in something useful and become the post-war generation of productive peace-time adults. Deborah's family was no exception. She was her parents' only child, born when her parents were both approaching their forties; to have started a family during the years of post-war austerity would not have been responsible, so by the time Deborah arrived there was no time for more pregnancies.

On a breezy spring morning as Deborah found the relevant page in her textbook on grammar, secretly relishing the next outpouring of didacticism, Mr Booth stared fixedly at a girl sitting at the back of the class, who seemed disengaged with the lesson and was gazing out of the window. The classroom had tall windows which looked out on the school grounds and beyond, where spring time clouds drifted across a pale blue sky.

'Young lady,' Mr Booth addressed the gazing girl, 'are you paying attention?'

'Sorry, sir,' replied the girl, 'I'm afraid I'm feeling rather sorry for myself today and I have forgotten my text book.' Mr Booth leant forward on the tall desk which resembled a pulpit behind which he perched to deliver his homilies, like a sermon.

'Do you think we would have won the war if we had felt sorry for ourselves in bomber command? Self-pity is odious. I have a spare text here which you may use. Write out one hundred times "I must never forget my English grammar or feel sorry for myself" and bring your labours to me before school tomorrow.' This was Mr Booth's standard form of discipline. The object of this admonition looked even more crestfallen as she sought the correct page in the text.

'Today we shall discuss gerunds.' Mr Booth announced. Deborah thought that this statement would not be quite accurate. There would be no discussion. Only Mr Booth was permitted to speak in his lessons.

For some reason this diversion stuck in Deborah's mind and she permanently associated gerunds with self-pity. More significantly she found that she agreed with Mr Booth's assertion that self-pity was odious and that was the only thing she retained from the lesson. Fifty years later she still had to resort to the dictionary to remind herself what a gerund is.

The post war generation, into which Deborah and her friends were born, had little cause for self-pity, even had they the inclination to indulge in the odious practice. They had not had to fight a war unless they wanted to join the forces; they grew up during the most liberal decades of the twentieth century in the security of their middle class comfort. Being mainly bright young women, they realised the expectations of their loving parents and invented useful careers for themselves.

Many years later, as she approached the age when she could contemplate retirement, Deborah had only one doubt; she had remained alone for all of her life. She had not managed to find a man, Jewish or gentile, with whom she was able to sustain a permanent relationship, and no one had found her. She had become resigned to her spinsterhood and refused to harbour regret, which she considered a pointless process on a par with the odiousness of self-pity

In the 1960's 'A' grades at 'A' level were almost unknown. A handful of prodigiously bright pupils at Deborah's school, usually the classicists, were dispatched to Baliol College at Oxford, on scholarships. The majority of Deborah's class obtained good enough grades to get them into the University of London or one of the renowned Northern universities from where they emerged three years later with first class degrees and offers of jobs in their chosen careers.

Deborah moved unfalteringly from school to University College in London, where she read English literature, and then applied to join the civil service, sailed through the protracted selection process and embarked on a life time career. She was a perspicacious young woman with a capacity to resolve complex situations. Her love of grammar was a metaphor for problem solving. The most complex problems became ordered under her supervision, like words in a perfectly grammatical sentence.

By the end of the 1970's Deborah was approaching thirty. She was slim, elegant and articulate. She retained the flawless complexion of her youth, her face dominated by large spectacles with colourful frames. She grew her straight, black hair to her shoulders and habitually scraped it back into a ponytail, which gave her a severe appearance. Her clarity of thought was an asset in her work; she became a high flier, regularly briefing junior and not so junior ministers and was serially promoted to more and more responsible roles.

Being the daughter of Jewish immigrant parents Deborah retained an awareness of what might have been had her parents not had the good fortune to escape from war time Europe and find a life in North London. Despite her success in her work, which might have made a less sensitive woman arrogant, she went through life with a sense of humility, realising success only through the strength of her own determination and innate intelligence. Her humility was sometimes seen as weakness among her competitive colleagues, but she knew it was an attribute which distinguished her from the pin-striped, over confident Whitehall men, with whom she was obliged to consort, and she cultivated it quietly along with her left-leaning political beliefs.

Through the eighties Deborah foresaw the tyranny which Thatcherism represented, the emergent creed of greed as a virtue and the atomising of society. She was not permitted to express her political views at work where they would have been condemned as subversive. She kept them carefully camouflaged only allowing them to emerge in private conversations with the series of men who sought her spirited company and her lissom body.

Men in general posed a problem for Deborah. She was not averse to their company but found the constant undertow of lasciviousness tiresome. Sex lurked beneath the surface of every social encounter, like an ice-berg waiting to ship wreck the occasion. Occasionally a man would entertain her with a semblance of gallantry, unabashedly relishing her company and humour, eschewing the subtext of the need for physical connection. Very occasionally she ended up in bed with these rare, empathetic men. But she had never found the means of shedding the tension which prevented her from relaxing sufficiently to abandon herself to the elusive sensations of which she knew she must be capable. Her attempts at sex became inextricably associated with disappointment. She remained stoically single.

Deborah was never lonely. She liked her own company and her restless intelligence was always a reliable source of entertainment. Being from a Jewish family her parents were ever present in her life and, when no other diversion distracted her, she would gravitate to her childhood home for Shabbat on Fridays, making excuses to her office and leaving before the daylight faded. This was the only manifestation of their religion in which her liberal-minded parents indulged. They found the gentle rituals of lighting candles and singing of blessings soothing. Her childhood bedroom was kept in a permanent state of readiness for her return, the Dodo poster still on the wall, which reminded her of the curious pedagogic inspiration of Mr Booth, which had embedded itself somewhere in the recesses of Deborah's organised mind.

The trajectory of the lives of Deborah and her parents was asymmetrical. As fast as Deborah advanced her career the lives of her parents declined. The poor health of both her father and mother obliged them to retire before they had intended. Their premature frailty caused Deborah great anxiety. They seemed to spend their lives between the local surgery and countless hospital appointments. Deborah's father died from a cancer, slowly and painfully, nursed by his wife, in his mid-sixties. Her mother died soon after, may be from grief but more probably from a heart attack. Before they died both had expressed their one regret; they had no grandchildren.

In her protracted state of grief Deborah distracted herself with work but knew that in reality she was escaping from an increasingly profound sadness and dissatisfaction. She reflected that she had never experienced hardship. Her life seemed to have been a series of achievements crowned with success and the security and comfort which a secure job and large salary provided. As the eighties advanced and the right wing policies of the decade secured ever greater wealth for the already wealthy and greater deprivation for the already deprived, her sense of disillusionment grew. The grandiose offices where Deborah conducted her high-ranking government business were a stone's throw from the squalor of social housing in which lived the unemployed and dispossessed. On her brisk progress from the tube station to her over heated office she had to step over the sleeping bodies of people lying on the pavement and in shop doorways. But the government which employed her denied that there was homelessness in Westminster. The hypocrisy of the decade started to undermine Deborah's sense of purpose. The lies to which she had to listen, peddled by the self-important politicians whom she was paid to advise, eroded the integrity of her belief in her own endeavours. The falsity and corruption which prevailed among the ruling classes seemed to have become part of the culture of the age. She let her disaffection be known. Very soon she was approached by an influential colleague who had been appointed to start one of the new 'think tanks' to research and advise on policy. Deborah resigned and hoped that a new direction would allow her to recover the self-respect which she relied upon to maintain her conscientious work ethic. Before she resigned she examined her motives to be certain that nowhere did self-pity influence her. Once satisfied that her motives were ethically sound and disinterested she happily vacated her powerful Whitehall edifice. Self-interest determined her decision, not self-pity. There was also the thought that new pastures might cultivate new men.

In her late thirties Deborah embarked on her new career. The 'think tank' to which she had been recruited had a high profile and obtained ready access to people and sources of information. The work brought her into contact with many new and distinguished people all of whom seemed to be anchored in marriages, middle class homes and varying numbers of children. She felt conspicuous in her comfortable, unattached life; clever, successful and attractive Deborah wondered if she intimidated men. To her list of accomplishments and qualities she resolutely added patient perseverance. Before she was forty she was determined that she would have a lover. Domesticity and children were not a priority but she needed a kind and intelligent man. Looking too hard for this paragon would not work. Time, fortune and coincidence would be her allies, and in due course, when she was least expecting it the object of her desire would materialise; and so he did.

At lunch times Deborah's regular haunt was the National Portrait Gallery. She liked to wander around the permanent exhibition seeking inspiration from the familiar faces of famous people gazing from their frames at the admiring public. One day she was looking closely at the names of people arrayed in military uniforms posing in a bizarre group portrait. She wondered if they had all had to stand for hours while the artist painted them or if they had been inserted individually in the composition. Next to the picture was a small plaque with an endless list of titles and honours of the subjects in the portrait. A bespectacled man with a receding hairline was also scrutinising the names of the serried ranks of military people. They stood close together, sharing each other's space, as people do in galleries. He turned to Deborah and pointed out a man in a grandiose uniform at the back of the picture.

'My great grandfather,' he said, 'responsible for the lives of innumerable soldiers whom he sent to be killed in the first war.' This announcement took Deborah by surprise. She had often stood uncomfortably close to other people in the gallery but never spoken to them.

'Did you know him?' She asked for want of anything else to say.

'No. Died before I was born. He was a sort of family legend for heroism. Ended up a general, but I looked him up the other day to find out exactly what he did. Then I discovered he was hanging here with all these exalted uniforms. Thousands of brave men died obeying his orders to attack the Germans. Not sure I would have agreed to be painted into history if I'd done what he did.' Deborah smiled at his cynicism and thought about her grandparents, victims of the holocaust, whom she had never known and had rarely been talked about. Perhaps they were more deserving of being memorialised than this decorated general. She was not sure she wanted to embark on this line of small talk with a stranger, so she said: 'Do you come to the gallery often?'

'Yes. Once or twice a week. I've seen you here before. My name's Collin. I work at Foyle's, selling books. Let me buy you a coffee or something at the café.' Deborah let herself be led to the overcrowded café wondering if Collin's approach was planned or opportunistic. Either way she thought there was nothing to lose and chatted benignly at Collin's observations about the public. He spoke rapidly about the many absurd encounters he had with the public in his work, peppering his commentary with literary allusions. Deborah found she enjoyed his banter. His voice had a deep resonance and lively intonation. He looked pleasant, clean shaven with intelligent eyes behind his rimless spectacles. He was evidently well informed about the authors of the books he sold and had an irreverent humour which made Deborah laugh. They drained their cappuccinos and Collin suggested they meet again. And so they did, every lunchtime and then in the evening at restaurants in Covent Garden. Deborah enjoyed the sense of being slowly seduced. She could not find a reason to resist the process and allowed their dates to become the basis of a relationship. They found out about each other, their work, politics, university, growing up in north London, and how in her thirties, Deborah was in search of a lover.

There would have to come a point when their congenial evenings would have to undergo the metamorphosis of getting into a bed together. Deborah tried to imagine Collin with no clothes on. He was tall and lean. She wondered if he was hairy. She reflected on how it would be to take off her clothes in his company and if she would be able to relax enough to abandon herself to whatever might come next. Although she knew she enjoyed his company, and liked the idea of being able to laugh at his humour, did she have the kind of affection for him which would make her want to be his lover; did she really trust him? The butt of much of his humour was the people he had to deal with every day. What did he really think about her? He had not made any affectionate noises which would suggest that he wanted to be physically close to her. There was another small seedling of doubt; Collin had never suggested going home together which is where she supposed they would need to go to become real lovers. In fact she knew very little about where Collin lived other than that he had a flat in North London. She decided to take a risk; she would suggest going back to his flat after their next restaurant assignation at the end of the week. Not very subtle, she thought, but she needed to know what was going to happen next.

They had their usual meal at a Covent Garden restaurant, conversational, funny and entertaining as it always was. The bill had arrived and they left their credit cards ready for the waiter to bring his machine.

'That was a lovely evening,' she said, 'when are we going to go home together?' Collin looked at her over his rimless spectacles and then perused the wine-stained tablecloth.

'I was hoping you wouldn't ask,' Collin replied quietly. 'I do really like being with you, but I'm married. My wife is a nurse and does nights a lot. That's why I'm available. She knows about you and seems to think it's OK. The marriage isn't great but we get along; we can't have kids which has been difficult.' He smiled weakly at her over his spectacles waiting for her response. Deborah could not believe she had been so gullible. All her analytical perspicacity, for which she was renowned in her work, had not provided her with the emotional antennae to realise that something was amiss. Suddenly she felt engulfed by sadness, dangerously like self-pity. There must be something wrong with her which made her so insensitive to what was going on around her. The humour which had beguiled her was no longer attractive, more like a defence against becoming emotionally closer; the bright, erudite conversation a smoke screen to avoid talking about their emotional selves. Then she felt like a fool; she had been prepared to get into a bed with this man, unclothed, find out if she could function sexually with him. A gulf of incomprehension seemed to impose itself between them. The waiter arrived and there was a short hiatus in their discomfort while he operated the card machine. She retrieved her card, found her bag and left without a word. She wandered out into the late, noisy Covent Garden streets feeling dejected, as if she were bereaved all over a again, and then angry at the deception to which she had been subjected.

That was the last time they met. Deborah felt humiliated and blamed herself for her myopic sensibilities which had made her incapable of perceiving the dissembling behaviour of a man to whom she had temporarily been prepared to give her naked self. She hated having ruminative, self-condemnatory thoughts which reminded her of Mr Booth's odious adage and the elusive gerund. Her own future was where she resided. Deborah's resolve to acquire a lover was undermined. She decided the future was herself, uncluttered by unreliable others.

A few days after the confessional meal she walked up the Charing Cross road, past the portrait gallery, as far as Foyle's. She wanted to know what Collin looked like from a distance; would he betray the flaw in his character which was not visible from close quarters. A longer perspective might give her a greater depth of field in which to view him. She found him in the fiction department and observed him from a distance, animatedly selling a book to a customer about whom he would no doubt laugh later, she thought cynically. She was careful not to be seen and left none the wiser. A café in the Charing Cross road provided refuge and time to ruminate. Deception was the most hurtful part of the whole encounter. The spontaneity of the original meeting had seemed to Deborah an ideal way to launch an affair. There had been nothing planned or contrived about their chance meeting in the gallery. Her trust in her own intuitive sense was badly undermined. She was confused about how she should have discovered the truth about Collin, long before she entertained the carnal thoughts of which she now felt ashamed. She resolved to seek a way to restore her self-esteem. The first thing was to abandon the captious notion that she needed a lover.

Years later, when Deborah was highly regarded by her professional colleagues, and had become an omniscient voice among the experts who thronged government think tanks and powerful committees, she reflected on whether life would have been substantially better had she not remained a single woman for the whole of her life. She was conscious of being a contented woman if not actually happy. She valued more than anything her own sharp intelligence which had guided her to success and respect. As the years went by she had involved herself in many causes championing the rights of women, liberty and oppressed minorities. But the abiding satisfaction in life had been the freedom to do what she wished to do, and the way in which she did it, whether acts of altruism or for her own fulfilment. She would never know whether the presence of a man in her life would have made the many good things which befell her better, but she could not really see how. Deborah never omitted to remember the most important imprecation of her youth – never to feel self-pity; neither could she see how being able to remember how gerunds worked would have changed anything for the better.

The Seduction of Celia

Celia had been a short-sighted child and wore spectacles from an early age. She preferred her spectacles to contact lenses because she liked the studious appearance with which they endowed her face, adding an academic appeal to her pale, flawless complexion, blue eyes and straight, dark hair. In her teens her parents paid eye-watering sums for colourful, designer spectacle frames, which was the only thing approaching a fashion statement which Celia allowed herself. She found the tight jeans and tops, which everyone wore, not very comfortable and unimaginative; they were like a uniform.

Celia liked to dress in cotton and linen. Loose cotton tops disguised her thinness. She mostly wore skirts of varying lengths. Occasionally she wore linen trousers. She realised that the way the trousers fitted betrayed the slimness of her waist and her small, shapely bum. She was as slim and lissom as any of her friends but she went to considerable lengths to keep her shape a secret.

Boys were not a priority in her life. A boyfriend had not materialised apart from one encounter with a boy from the year above at her North London school. She had spent long periods of time with him lying on her back being kissed, which made her mouth sore. He was the first person to tell her that she had a fascinating scent, which he found exciting. At the time she did not understand the significance of this observation. She never wore perfume and thought cosmetics were what older people used to disguise their blemished skin.

When she started at university she was still a virgin. Celia had been a model pupil at school and been rewarded with spectacular 'A' levels and a place at King's College, in the University of London, to read law.

Sacrificing the comfortable anchorage of her parents' home in North London for the noise and squalor of a student residence seemed illogical. She was an only child and her parents were delighted to go on having their precious, clever daughter at home.

'Darling, you know we love having here,' said her Mum, 'you must feel free to come and go as you want.'

At first Celia had been overwhelmed by the volume of reading and assignments which she was expected to keep up with. Gradually she learnt the language of the law. Skilful tutoring gave her confidence and she started to look at the non-academic opportunities available to her on the campus. She acquired a low key social life and started to notice her fellow students. They were a clever, diverse group, more women than men. Many of them were from the Asian community, and like Celia, continued to live with their parents. Her tutorial group of five girls, all Asian, wore pastel coloured scarves wrapped tightly round their heads, concealing the dark tresses of hair beneath. One day, before the tutorial began, one of the girls produced a pale, blue cotton scarf from her bag. She laid it on Celia's head and arranged it, like her own, concealing Celia's hair.

'That's better. Now you are a good Muslim girl. Don't smile at the boys or your father will keep you at home,' she advised. The group dissolved in giggles but the gesture was one of acceptance and friendship. Celia wore the scarf to all the tutorials.

Celia had great powers of concentration and a retentive memory, uncompromised by the regular immersion in alcohol, which many of her peers regarded as a necessary part of life. Her intellect suited her perfectly to study law. At the end of the first year she came top in the end of term exams and won a prize.

During the long vacation Celia met her old school friends, stayed for two weeks in a Gite in Normandy with her parents, and studied. She returned to the law faculty with renewed confidence after her exam success. She started to be noticed by the academic staff and the other students as a rising star. Celia was expert at making herself invisible and had gone unnoticed until she came top of her class.

On a summer afternoon she was conscientiously reading the judgement of some common law precedent in the library. One of the post-graduate law students sat down opposite Celia and gazed at her intrusively until she looked at him. Then he pushed a piece of paper across the table to her; talking was not permitted in the library. Celia read the message in neat hand-writing: Buy you a drink. 5.00pm in the bar? Celia peered through her colourful spectacle frames at the source of this invitation. She had seen him before in the department but did not know who he was. She smiled shyly and nodded. In due course she tidied up her books and packed her copious notes in the bag she carried with her. Her admirer had disappeared some time ago. She walked pensively to the student bar and found her host who was alone, installed behind a pint glass. Celia hesitantly accepted a glass of wine and they sat together by a window overlooking the Strand.

'I'm Brian,' said her companion, 'thanks for coming. Please don't get me wrong but I've been watching you. I think you're very pretty. Everyone knows you're very clever. All you need is a sense of humour and you'll be the most desirable girl in the law school.' Celia blushed. Flattery was something she had never sought and never received. She was uncertain what to make of this approach.

She looked at her companion. He had short, dark hair and brown eyes. His face was pleasing and he smiled when he saw he was being assessed. He was casually dressed in a green shirt and black jeans.

'I've never really thought about it.' Celia managed to say. 'I suppose I don't really like being noticed.'

'I think that's what makes you interesting, to me at least. Why would someone as appealing as you not want to attract attention, like everyone else?'

Celia thought a moment. 'Perhaps because I'm not everyone else.'

Brian appraised her and nodded. 'No. I think that must be right, which of course makes you even more fascinating. Would you let me take you out somewhere, a restaurant, theatre; whatever you'd like to do.' Celia was unsure what to make of this either. Despite her half-hearted attempts to socialise she had never been asked out by a member of the opposite sex. She sat very straight in her chair holding on to her glass.

'But I've never met you before. I don't know who you are.' She thought she sounded naïve, which she did. Brian seemed to find this amusing and laughed briefly. Celia thought she was being laughed at and bridled visibly.

'I'm sorry, Celia. I love the way you react. I thought maybe we could get to know each other at a restaurant. What do you think? Where do you like?' Celia looked at Brian carefully. He was nice looking and sounded earnest in his intention. He is a lawyer, she thought, surely I can trust him and immediately realised the naivety of her assumption.

Celia relented. 'I like Covent Garden,' she said.

'Perfect. We can walk there and there's plenty of places which won't break the bank. Let me take you out – please,' he added pleadingly. Celia smiled at his perseverance. She thought she should feel flattered but was unsure what was supposed to happen.

'Let's go,' said Brian and he stood up assertively. Celia let herself be taken. The early evening streets were warm and full of people hurrying somewhere. They sauntered to the edge of Covent Garden where the atmosphere was changed by crowds of dawdling tourists looking at shops. They chatted easily about what they had in common at the law school; the students, tutorials, the tutors, Brian's complex studies for his Master's degree and Celia's ambitions. They found a small dark restaurant and ate chicken and couscous. Celia had a second glass of wine knowing that it would make her feel peculiar. She became more voluble, which appealed to Brian, who had already become besotted with her presence and chaste naivety.

After Brian had gallantly paid the bill he said; 'Let's do this again. I love your company.' Celia agreed to meet him again in two days' time and find another restaurant. As they parted company Brian embraced her gently and kissed her briefly on each cheek.

'I'm sure I'm not the first person to say this to you, Celia,' he ventured, 'but you do smell delicious.' He was the second person to inform Celia of this dubious attribute. She did not respond and headed for Leicester Square tube to get the Northern Line home. She sat miserably in the train. She was appalled. She did not want to smell of anything and made significant efforts not to.

When she got home she undressed and got in the shower. She rinsed herself carefully all over, without using soap, and dried with equal care. She slid naked beneath her huge Duvet, enjoying the sensation of coolness. Then she pulled the Duvet over her head, curled herself up, and inhaled deeply. There was a smell of clean sheet, and something else; a faint, sweet, feral smell which she had not noticed before. It appealed to her but she could not work out where it came from. She tried to sniff at her armpits and smell her small breasts, all of which seemed odourless. She put her hand between her legs and pressed a finger inside until she felt wetness. She brought her hand close to her nose and sniffed at her finger. The smell, which she liked, was different and more pungent than the other aroma. She cautiously licked her moist finger in the darkness under the duvet with the tip of her tongue. It tasted salty. May be it was something to do with her skin. She wondered if she had glands somewhere which produced this elusive scent which excited men. Then she fell asleep wondering if it was an atavistic aphrodisiac to attract the opposite sex. The idea did not appeal to her.

Brian and Celia continued to see each other at regular intervals in a mainly Platonic way. Brian had decided that he must be patient and allow Celia time to get to like him enough before thinking about sharing his bed. He had become obsessed with Celia, to whose sensual skin he had been permitted limited access, and her intoxicating scent which aroused him. He ceased to mention how enticing her smell was as he realised that she did not like the idea of smelling of anything, however alluring.

During Celia's third year at university she had her twenty-first birthday. Brian chose this occasion for the seduction of Celia and took her back to his bed-sit where he produced a bottle of champagne. Celia had foreseen this and decided that Brian had been kind, attentive and generous for long enough; may be it was right to take their relationship a step further, but she was ambivalent about giving up her carefully preserved virginity. The champagne did not help. It made Celia feel peculiar as alcohol usually did. When she had recovered enough from the effects of the champagne, and feeling slightly disinhibited, she allowed Brian to divest her of her clothes, item by item, until the only thing she wore was her spectacles, a process she found funny and exciting. Celia unclothed was beautiful, something which she alone knew, and had never shared.

Brian was dazzled by her small breasts, narrow waist and slim legs. He shed his own clothes in a hurry and embraced Celia beneath the duvet with the gentle reverence he felt for her. He whispered blandishments about his amazement at Celia's physical perfection. Celia was rigid with anxiety and no amount of soothing allowed her to relax. She was still a virgin in the morning.

'It doesn't matter,' Brian reassured her. 'It takes time to get used to being in bed together.' Celia was mortified. She told Brian, as gently as she could, that she did not want to see him again. She was embarrassed by what she perceived to be her own failure to function sexually. Brian was distraught but Celia was adamant. She removed herself from the social scene of the College and cocooned herself in the only thing at which she was confident that she could excel; learning about the law.

The months passed and Celia was approaching the end of her time as an undergraduate. It was inevitable that she qualified with a first class degree and more prizes. Her professor tried to entice her into becoming an academic lawyer but Celia had decided that she was going to specialise in human rights law. The law fascinated her. Human rights offered an altruistic direction; the possibility of being able to represent people whose need was desperate, something which other branches of the law did not seem to offer.

Celia launched herself on the job market. Her complexion, her perfect, virginal body and her academic achievement made her flawless; she was articulate, clear thinking and passionate about her ambition. Despite her lack of experience of the world she was inundated with offers from law firms to take her on. She became articled to a high profile solicitor in her chosen specialty in a law firm near Fleet Street.

During the following years Celia continued to live with her parents and immersed herself in her work. She was offered a partnership with the law firm on her twenty-ninth birthday. With partnership came realistic earnings and she started to rent a flat in Bloomsbury from where she could easily walk to work. She became increasingly well known in the community of lawyers who practiced human rights law; she was clever, attractive and had a quiet sense of humour. She became a lodestar among the lascivious young barristers with whom she worked and received countless invitations to parties and dinners. Occasionally she permitted herself tentative intimacies with some of the more ardent young men, but knew intuitively when her feral aroma aroused her companion which immediately made her feel tense. She was certain that she would not be able to reciprocate their advances.

When she was thirty-five Celia embarked on a relationship with a barrister ten years her senior, called Edward. He had been particularly supportive of her work for the numerous dispossessed people whose rights Celia attempted to represent. Edward walked with a limp as a result of a serious traffic accident five years previously, in which his wife had been killed. He had spent two days unconscious in hospital. His appearance was well groomed and conventional. He was a man of great integrity which appealed to Celia. She found their evenings spent in restaurants around Fleet Street and the Strand more congenial than the company of the pin-striped Lotharios.

One evening they were sheltering in the doorway of a Fleet Street restaurant with the freezing, February rain pelting the pavement, waiting for a vacant taxi. Edward drew Celia towards him and softly embraced her. Celia became aware of a sense of languid arousal, which took her by surprise. She melted in his embrace. Edward breathed her in.

'I wish I knew what you smelled like, Celia,' he whispered, 'ever since I banged my head in the accident I've not been able to smell a thing.'